Properties
of
Blood

Books by William Mills

Poetry

Watch for the Fox
Stained Glass
The Meaning of Coyotes

Fiction

I Know a Place: Stories
Those Who Blink: A Novel
Properties of Blood: Stories

Criticism

The Stillness in Moving Things:
    The World of Howard Nemerov

Non-Fiction

Bears and Men: A Gathering
    (Text & Photographs)
The Arkansas: An American River
    (Text & Photographs)
Louisiana Cajuns
    (Introductory Text)

Properties of Blood

Stories by

William Mills

THE UNIVERSITY OF ARKANSAS PRESS
FAYETTEVILLE 1992

This book was designed by Ellen Beeler using the typeface Simoncini
Garamond.

The paper used in this publication meets the minimum requirements of
the American National Standard for Permanence of Paper for Printed
Library Materials Z39.48-1984. ⊚

LIBRARY OF CONGRESS CATALOGING-IN-PUBLICATION DATA

Mills, William, 1935–
      Properties of blood: stories / by William Mills.
          p. cm.
      ISBN 1-55728-243-9 (alk. paper). —ISBN 1-55728-244-7
      (pbk.: alk. paper)
      I. Title.
      PS3563.I4234P76   1992
      813'. 54--dc20
                                                          91-29773
                                                          CIP

Some of these stories have appeared in *The Southern Review, The New
Orleans Review, The Cimarron Review, Selected Stories from* The Southern
Review: 1965–1985, *Mississippi Writers: Reflections of Childhood and
Youth, Chronicles,* and *Something in Common: Contemporary Louisiana
Stories.* "Mr. Bo" was first printed in 1969 by Loyola University, New
Orleans. Reprinted by permission of the *New Orleans Review.*

For James Whitehead
and again for Bev

CONTENTS

Sweet Tickfaw Run Softly, Till I End My Song

⁘

Fred Carlisle first sensed the danger like a rhino might who
has foraged too close to killer bees protecting the center of
the hive. Like a humming or buzzing that was unnoticed
until the sound became stronger, then certain. He knew his
immune-response system was outnumbered and that his
little cells of resistance were being subtly overcome, so he
scratched the thick hair on his chest and headed to the
refrigerator for another beer, just a little sooner than he normally would have. He was outgunned by females five to one.

Ever since his wife had run off with the resident hematol-
ogist (met through his own good offices, Carlisle being the
head X-ray technician), he had taken up the guitar. With

that special fecklessness of the newly divorced, he took to the beaches, or rather a longish sand bar on the river Tickfaw, with his sailor hat, six beers, and the guitar. He felt himself alternately the sad buffoon and the troubadour, depending on the effect of the beer and the sun. The troubadour is not easy to bring off when one is absolutely alone. Parents see to it that their children get nowhere near. Or, consider the dark repulsion, the dank specter, that arises in the minds of young men and women alike when, already nearly denuded for the sun and water, they suddenly confront a solitary, hairy-chested fellow strumming his guitar and singing softly to the river. Why has he come out from the shadows where he surely must reside? Imagine though how this force field would change about if one other human, man, woman, or child, were sitting by the singer's side, listening. The children would be permitted to gather round, for then the piper's goat feet would appear to be only sandaled toes. The sleepy, sun-drowsed young men and women would then envy the artist for his resemblance to the happy figures in the soft-drink ads on television—instead of the kind of figure that might lurk around bus-station restrooms.

Carlisle's loneliness was about to get him all the way down so that he could not even sing alone, when one afternoon two young, succulent junior divinities wandered near him, and the younger (both were less than half his age) asked innocently, "What kind of guitar is that?" Before either could get away, he thrust his instrument toward his inquisitor. "Swedish. Do you play?"

"No," the younger one continued. "My father used to."

"He doesn't play anymore?"

"He lives someplace else now." She fondled the neck of the guitar "His was Mexican. I thought most guitars came from Mexico and Spain."

"I got this one when I was in the army. I was on vacation and went to Sweden and saw it there." Both of the girls had those well-developed, muscular bodies that had taken Carlisle's breath away when he was stationed in Germany. Much to be said for active women he thought.

Though Carlisle had had no children, he thought he understood Lot's difficulties with his daughters. Like most men, as he had gotten older he had to account for his lust for girls who had not yet crossed the Greenwich Mean Line of Womanhood. His meditations on this led him to the obvious conclusion that the lust was perfectly natural—and that it must be fought like the true confrontation with the Devil it was—a Devil that threatened town and family, the civilized life.

Carlisle did not have long to flail his lust out of mind (as his eyes roved the dark tans of their flat abdomens and as they shook their long hair insouciantly), for just then an older, less tanned model was hieing it over the sand a bit clumsily, her soft thighs having fallen sullenly from an earlier grace.

So it was that the river Tickfaw became the setting for this union of the divorced. Several weeks passed by, and Carlisle had "taken up" with this *Schatz* of German descent, Karola Mummelthey, and her offsprings (a funny word) Veila and Veronica. His pitch on the beach had been a response to her pitch: the plumbing and appliances were breaking down because they had bought everything new when they had married but now it was sixteen years and a woman had no preparation for fixing such things, always thinking her job was elsewhere—and Carlisle's had been a dignified and appropriate, "I have always been good with my hands."

By the time Karola's sister showed up with husband for a two-day visit some three months later, Carlisle had become a cog in the domestic machine. He encouraged his mate to cook German food for he perceived her as a German when she had in fact been born and reared in Des Moines. Such cooking was news to her, but Carlisle tried to infect her with the idea that it was going back to roots. She sniffed at this, but fell into German potato salad, kraut, and fresh pork sausages that were dubbed bratwurst, and whatever else fitted his notion of things German. (How many Chinese have arrived in the States and been invited to cook Peking Duck or other elegances and, never having eaten them themselves, had to turn to in quick fashion?)

Veila and Veronica were just tickled pink having a man around who could fix bicycles and run them to Girl Scouts and run them to the Y.W.C.A. and so on—were pink for about two months until the newness wore off and Karola brought him in as a consultant disciplinarian.

The Mother: "Shouldn't they be in bed by nine-thirty?" "Tell them they're too young to be wearing Tropicana Red lipstick."

The Disciplinarian: "OK, you girls do what your mother says."

What comes next, of course, is "You're not our daddy."

Carlisle sighed. Would that they could be with this phantom, Frederick Rodehorst. They had kept his name. He still sometimes sent money. Karola Mummelthey would have no more of Rodehorst. She had spent a week changing social security, credit cards, bank accounts. Then she found out she had no credit. Carlisle was glad he wasn't around when she found that out. Her old man could still rile what was left of that *Deutches Blut.* That was another thing: the surfeit of names around the house. Carlisle, Mummelthey, Rodehorst. What to do? A school friend comes by and says "Hello Mr. Rodehorst." Carlisle just lets it go. Too much trouble explaining everything. A lot of the time you just have to let things ride. But the girls speak up. "His name is not Rodehorst. It's Carlisle." The school friend looks askance of somebody. "Their daddy is in New York City." So the friend figures right. She's got that under control. Then the girls' mother walks in and she gets the "Hello Mrs. Rodehorst."

"Honey, my name is Mrs. Mummelthey. My girls' name is Rodehorst, after their father." It's not long before the kid gets on her bicycle and tools right out of this madhouse where nobody seems to have the right name. Even having the same first name as Rodehorst bothered Carlisle. He could never be sure when Karola murmured "Oh Fred" during love time whether she had impaled herself on the nothink of ecstasy and was simply replying with the name she had murmured for sixteen years. He had once thought of asking her to murmur "Carlisle," but he knew that wouldn't cut it. Although it did have a German formality about it.

What's in a lot of names? Confusion. And the grid was upped just a hair when Karola's sister and her husband putted into the driveway in an ancient Citroen. Sheila was the sister's name, but no longer Mummelthey. Rather Polowski after her husband, Oskar Polowski. A second generation Pole. He and Sheila still lived in Des Moines with their twelve-year-old daughter, Tammy Sue. Tammy Sue Polowski had pain-in-the-ass written across her face to be read in any language.

Both of them were interested to see about this "new man in Karola's life." She had no doubt written them. Carlisle was interested in them, too. With his intense desire to know about people and their native lands, he had read up on Poles. He had even asked Karola if she would cook some native Polish food, but she said enough was enough and that she had heard it wasn't any good. She wrinkled her nose.

Sheila Polowski was a year younger than Karola. And it may have been that or the one child less, but she was taut as a drum and had a watchfulness about her that said her radar was always on full alert. She was, however, a little splay-eyed, and it was hard to tell sometimes which eye to look at when she looked at you. Carlisle knew that she was good to look at. She had a habit of keeping the tip of her tongue wet and then caressing her lower lip. This was when she looked at him. She was friendly and all right. So was Oskar. He was six-by-six, and when he shook Carlisle's hand it was like having a warm pot roast thud across his palm. He was in plumbing fixtures in Des Moines, so Carlisle had something to talk about with him straight away. Thirty minutes and a cold beer later, they were seated on the tub edge and commode respectively, discussing a new trap that had come out which would put a stop to the commode's leak.

During dinner that first evening (Mummelthey tipping her hat at least with crisp, thin wiener schnitzel) their vacation plans came out and it seemed they were leaving after one more night to go to New Mexico. Why New Mexico?

"TM" said Sheila softly. Oskar looked away embarrassed.

"TM?" echoed Carlisle.

"Transcendental Meditation."

With the smoothness of a right-hand arpeggio on his guitar, Carlisle played the host (played the guest?). "Oh, I've wanted to talk to somebody who knew something about that. What's it about?"

Oskar looked just the slightest bit surprised, as if Carlisle had evidenced an interest in knitting bootees, but he kept his counsel as Sheila went on. "I've just really gotten into it, just scratched the surface, and that's why I'm going to this TM camp in Taos. But it's a way to get in touch with your inner self."

"I see. Sounds interesting."

Karola was nodding approvingly. She was a very affirmative person. If a friend or sister said she was going to join the Foreign Legion, she would nod vigorously, then later on ask what the Foreign Legion was. Someone was going to surf on a tidal wave . . . nod, nod. Going to grow babies from butterfly manure . . . nod, nod.

"Do you find it pretty helpful, Oskar?" inquired Carlisle.

"Oh, I haven't gotten into it yet," he said respectfully.

"Oskar is going to go hiking with Tammy Sue while Sheila goes to the camp," explained Karola. The two sisters had been discussing all this while Oskar and Carlisle had worked on the commode.

Oskar grinned a little sheepishly. "I never cared for that kind of stuff," meaning TM, no doubt, for he got a sharp little look from Sheila.

"I've tried to get Oskar interested in something to develop his potential, but it's hard to get a Polack to change his ways."

Oskar didn't grin at this. Oh, well, thought Carlisle, another happy marriage. The Prussians were partitioning Poland again. Carlisle had read about the sorrow that was Poland. Everybody wanted a piece of it. Christ's body, he thought. A polish sausage, he thought.

Karola got up to make coffee, but Carlisle asked Oskar if he wouldn't like another drink, and Oskar said yes, he would, and did he have any gin. Carlisle felt sympathetic to Oskar, and as the evening passed and they drank more and more, Carlisle pulled out his guitar and the two men hacked up a few old American favorites, and then Carlisle showed off his two German songs, *"Der Wirtin Tochterlein,"* and *"So Ist's."*

"Fred's a lot more German than we are, Sheila." And with that Karola took Oskar's glass to refill it, and he followed her to the kitchen.

"You really sing those very well," Sheila said, putting that tip of her tongue just between her lips and then wetting the bottom one. Carlisle thanked her. "I really envy you and Karola's life-style," she said, "You both seem so free."

"Absolutely true, absolutely," bubbled Carlisle. What a wonderfully free life he had. What nice folks the Polowskis are. How good booze was. "Yes, my little *Schatzy,* there's no denying our great and free passion."

She looked deeply into Carlisle's eyes as if searching for an answer.

"Sheila, let me get you a drink," urged Carlisle, getting up. She had not been drinking.

"No, I'm fine," but she got up with him to go to the kitchen.

"A great little sister you got here," Carlisle said to Karola, and as he did so, Sheila laughed and put her arm around his waist and gave him a little squeeze.

"Watch it, little sister," Karola said, teasingly. Oskar became related to the three of them from outside, a separate point looking at a triangle. Sheila continued to hold him around the waist, now a little longer than was seemly.

"Another drink, Oskar?" moving to the refrigerator, leaving Sheila to stand.

"No, I 'bout had enough. It was a long drive."

Before Karola dropped off to sleep, she delivered the domestic news report. "They're having trouble." And Carlisle sighed, not knowing what else to do.

At breakfast Oskar and Sheila wore faces with criss-crossed marks of sleepless anger. Carlisle felt a pang of sadness that he did not show, but he remembered lying in that special cauldron feigning sleep for hours whether too proud or too indecisive to leave the bed. He could remember that, but just as truly, he felt outside (not really above) their troubles. He had done his time hadn't he? There was the distance and amusement of the old soldiers watching the new recruits. You ain't seen nothing yet, buddy. There is an airy omipotence that accompanies this distance if one's memory is not especially vivid.

Carlisle left everyone at the table talking about Des Moines and made a dead run for the apartment that he still kept near the hospital. This was his Saturday for duty, and he had to slip into a fresh set of whites. During the day he called Karola and suggested they go to a riverside seafood dine-and-dance establishment—working-class style. She remarked sort of secretly that, yes, it would probably be good if everyone got out and loosened up.

The work day went easily, with Saturday always being for non-scheduled shots that could not be done during the regular week. One chick needed several shots of her skull. Later in the afternoon she came walking back in the office and asked him if she could see the X-rays. It was against the rules unless the physician wanted to show them to her, but she had big tits and he knew she wouldn't understand the negatives anyway. She gasped, seeing beyond her lips and cheeks and hair for the first time. But what appalled her the most were the massive spots where her teeth were—she had about twenty fillings which generally were invisible even to her. Naturally she asked about the tumor, but Carlisle answered he didn't know how to interpret X-rays. Partly a lie. Besides getting him in trouble with the radiologist, it was better for her to be more concerned about the surface of things, instead of that hazy presence that might well spell the transition from tits and lips to dust. Looking beneath the surface of things was not all it was cracked up to be. The patterns were there, the symmetry. But what was always of such interest to people spelled a lot of trouble.

Carlisle felt expansive driving to Mummelthey's. He had changed to a blue chambray work shirt and white dungarees. He felt watery—maritime, bawdy and yo-ho-ho. Karola had felt the evening out would loosen everybody up, and Carlisle agreed. They ordered piles of hot, steaming shrimp in the shells and hardshell crabs. Peeling and cracking all that succulence lent a fine sensuality to the day. They had cold mugs of beer, and immediately afterward, chilled bottles of blanc de blanc. The Polowskis seemed to get into the spirit of things. The drinking helped. Sheila was enjoying the cool wine, now and then drinking deeply. Without any

9

special effort it seemed Oskar talked mostly to Karola, and this left Carlisle with Sheila. Carlisle kept her glass always filled, being a great believer in the release of anxiety through euphoria, induce it how you will. Dionysus soon led them to the big, dark dancehall on the river. One of the things that Carlisle felt he could hold onto in a world that was as slippery as eels—a treacherous world where wealthy hematologists could raid hospital staff, promising their wives Mercedes—was the body of woman. He dearly loved the electric interface of locked male and female ventral sides, tits to chest, pelvis to pelvis, that atomic bond as he pulled a woman's lower spine, her tailbone, closer to him. And he did this night. He danced with Karola and danced a lot with Sheila. Oskar Polowski did not feel the Nureyev wings that Carlisle felt tonight. Apparently. While Oskar was dancing with Karola, Carlisle was left at the table with the wine-tuned Sheila. Can a chief X-ray technician find happiness with his girlfriend's sister from Des Moines, a second generation *Schatz*? Yes. And so could she. Later as she murmured "Oh, wonderful," she grasped (in the dark) his male instrument. Not his guitar, either.

What a joy! Barnacle Carlisle having this happen to him in the dark. But what a fright! His girl friend's sister. A fellow Mummelthey! The barnacled Nureyev danced on with Polowski née Mummelthey thinking how surely the sibilancy of sin issued from the serpent's hiss. And her soft tongue that had moistened her lip now moistened his. A straightforward joy.

So far so good? All the people go home from their frolic, and the Polowskis wheel it for the heights of New Mexico next morning: one to transcend via the spirit, and the other using his two feet. A duality with one appendage, a daughter that has the look of an imp. All in a Citroen.

Back to the rhythm of the household. What's in an interlude? Only a memory and one that he hopes does not announce itself if he should talk in his sleep. Family life, roll on, roll on. A little discipline for the Rodehorsts (on request from their mother), nice candlelight suppers in the evening after a day spent working at his profession, searching for cloudy spots or irregularities beneath the surfaces of the people who have been sent to X-ray.

During a nice supper of sauerbraten and potato salad, one week after the Citroen had left, the phone goes off. Veila calls to her mother to pick up on the extension in the dining room. Carlisle tries not to let all of his attention leave the food but cannot help being distracted by Karola's end of the conversation. It is her sister.

"I know, I know," and she is nodding. "Don't cry. It's going to be all right. Look at me." She nods some more. "You know I will . . . right, right, don't let anyone push you around . . . you don't have to put up with it . . . sure you can come here, you know you can. You just get on the plane and come right out here. Forget the car. Let him go climbing around in the mountains . . . OK . . . can't wait to see you again."

Mummelthey was very excited. "They're having trouble. I told you. Sheila has left him." Carlisle went on eating, trying to figure out how this was going to change his life. He knew things don't ever stay the same, as much as you want them to, and he wondered what boded his way now. Mummelthey repeated much of the conversation that he had already guessed.

"Maybe this is just a little fight," he offered. "She's not leaving him for anybody else, right?"

"No, of course not. He just won't support her emotionally in the way that she needs. He imprisons her."

"He seemed like a nice sort to me," volunteered Carlisle.

That seemed to stop her a moment. She really liked Oskar. Had always thought he was a Gibraltar for her sister.

11

This only served to confuse her. But she came back finally with, "Oh, you men always stick together." What man did he stick together with, Carlisle wondered?

All the next morning while they waited for the plane, Carlisle was struck with the almost jubilant excitement that had come over Mummelthey. It didn't seem the appropriate feeling for a breakup. More a festive air. Karola had taken special care with her hair and face this morning and put on one of the dresses he favored because it made her look quite sensual. In a modest way.

The remainder of the day was a great emotional drain like the day of a funeral or a trip to the dentist. Both of the sisters thrived on it. And mixed in this alloy was Carlisle's own curiosity about what Sheila was thinking about since she had grabbed his dong at the dance. Maybe she had forgotten? Maybe that had helped bring her back here? No. Hummmm. For a moment he put his arm affectionately around her shoulders while Mummelthey fixed supper and she leaned thankfully against him with Mummel looking on happily. Carlisle thought, look, this is the twentieth century. Maybe he could just shepherd both women and their offsprings. *Ménage à trois*? Just then her little brat daughter walked in, glared at him, tugged at her mother's arm, and pulled her loose from Carlisle. "Mother, why can't Daddy come back with us?"

"Because we are going to live separately. But you can see him anytime you want. Karola, how far off is supper?"

"Twenty minutes."

"Could you make it thirty?"

"Sure. What's up?"

"I generally meditate at this time."

Everybody got still for an instant. Embarrassed silence.

"Sure, sure," nodded Mummelthey.

What's a fine, sensual *Schatz* who grabs dongs in the dark

doing in an empty room all locked away: After she left, Carlisle suggested to her kid, "Why don't you meditate a little in your room like your mother?" The kid stuck her tongue out. She didn't have the same movement with her tongue as her mother, but she left anyway.

"Why did you do that?" demanded Mummelthey.

"Nothing. Just kidding." He got a narrowed look. Forget the *ménage à trois*.

After supper the three adults sat around the table. They talked divorce. It seemed like a woman's affair. They laid plans just like he remembered hearing his wife lay plans for his marriage.

"You can move in here until you get settled," Mummelthey offered her sister. Didn't ask Carlisle, *danseur extraordinaire* and guitarist.

"Oh, but Fred would feel too cramped with so many women," and then she did her number with the tongue between the lips, batting her eyelashes.

"I'll levitate you," thought Carlisle. "I'll send you transcending with my instrument." Aloud, though, "Of course not. Just one big happy family." Mummelthey knew he was lying and she got piqued. He got up and got some gin. Veila came into the kitchen screaming that Veronica had slapped her because she and Tammy Sue Polowski wanted to be alone in her bedroom.

"If you girls don't learn to love one another, Fred is going to give you a licking," Mummelthey threatened. The screaming stopped, and Carlisle sighed. He didn't like being represented as lawgiver or domestic enforcer. There was getting to be this new level of buzzing, buzzing around the old pad. Polowskis and Rodehorsts in the bedroom, and Polowskis and Mummeltheys in the kitchen.

"This will all blow over, Sheila," counseled Carlisle. "You'll probably be back in your lover's arms by week's end." This was not a popular thing to say he discovered. They had already started laying plans for the divorce. They didn't want the wife left standing at the court bench.

"Oh you just don't know what living with him is like, Fred. He's not interested in the spirit, in the adventure of discovering one's identity. He just says he already knows who he is, Oskar Polowski." Her look was intense, and her eyes smouldered. "He doesn't support me in developing who I am."

You've developed a pretty fast right hand in the dark, honey. First things first. A hand, a quick tongue, and then a quick soul. "What would you do that's any different than with Oskar?" This kind of talk killed any playful flirting that had been going on between Sheila and him. Analysis did it every time. Like an X-ray of Marilyn Monroe. Not too good to forget the surfaces of things.

"I can't get him interested in anything like meditation. He's so set in his ways."

"You mean he won't do what you want him to do." A shot across the bow.

"Fred," howled Mummelthey. "How cruel! You know that's not what she means." There'd be no cavorting tonight.

"Maybe so," he murmured. "I just hate to see you split. Maybe just lay out for a while. Forget the institution thing. How can you make love when you're an institution. Maybe if marriage could become a loose confederation of states rather than a federal institution, then maybe you could levitate, and . . . "

"It's not levitate, Fred," Mummelthey cut in.

" . . . and Oskar could be into plumbing fixtures and hiking. And you just gird up the confederacy when it is threatened from without, but when the threats are gone, back to doing what you can, or like to do. If maybe folks just confederated by choice and by the threat of outside invasion just so they could have more time for balling and thinking

14

and dreaming, then the confederation would stay loose. And if we spent as much vigilance staying loose as we do girding up for outside threats, there'd be plenty of time for just having fun." Fred Carlisle was suddenly embarrassed about his speech. And it had dashed all the divorce ceremonies for the moment, or at least the momentum. "I just hate to see you dissolve if you don't have to, and furthermore, I am going outside with my guitar. You girls continue to march."

It's not just that way, though, is it, he thought? A loose confederation was not just a dream, it could happen (look at Mummelthey and him, look at the 1780s in the States), but just as surely, it was only a point on a curve, like the sine wave on his oscilloscope at the lab. And just as surely there were the partitions of Poland. He took his guitar and sat out on the imitation redwood picnic table in the patio, strummed a few chords, and began to sing. The neighbor slammed his window down, but Carlisle kept on singing and thinking—sometimes of the beach on Tickfaw River, but mostly of a horny woman sitting on the ground in a lotus position trying to transcend time, and of Polowski high in the mountains in New Mexico.

Belle Slough

Adam struggled his way up through darkness to the light. Clay Calloway, his hunting buddy and host, had opened the door to the hall, allowing the soft light in. Clay didn't have to say anything, just went into the kitchen to start coffee. They had to meet some other hunters an hour before first light. Being awakened at three in the morning was hard enough, and Adam felt grateful that he and Clay were past the age of horseplay, the kind he remembered in army barracks and at college. That would have made the early hour even harder.

They had gone to bed early. In spite of a couple of bourbons they still turned in at a decent hour. He noticed he was doing that differently now too. Getting older was odd. He mostly did the same things and felt no differently inside, but being fifty subtly changed things. He was not always able to put his finger on the changes, but they were there. One thing he knew certainly, he ached more when he first got up and sometimes at the end of the day.

There were probably more ducks in Louisiana where Adam often hunted, but he had come to Arkansas for the reason many men hunt anyway, the companionship. For several years he had stopped hunting and spent his time taking pictures of wildlife. Taking pictures outdoors led one to do some of the same things hunting required—both took you outside where it was important whether there was rain or snow, clouds or bright sun. One had to get to know the birds and animals better in order to get closer to them for a picture. Adam liked to take pictures. The craft compelled him to pay attention to light. It mattered very much whether a bird was backlit or not, whether the creature was in overhead light that left no shadows, or in the many shades of red and yellow as the earth turned first towards its sun, and later away.

Yet taking pictures was not the same. There was not the sense of completeness one had after a successful hunt. Also, if the weather was dark or rainy, the photographer didn't go out. With hunting, especially with the short seasons allowed by game laws, one had to hunt when it was time. Or not hunt at all. With duck hunting the weather was almost always cold and as often as not included rain.

The truth was, he sometimes hated to get up early, like this morning, and wondered why he did it. It was like a ritual, though, and once it was time for the ritual to begin, it had to begin. Once it was under way, especially after first light, then Adam knew he was right to have come.

He put on thermal long johns, then a thick wool shirt, next two pair of wool socks and his insulated overalls. The overalls were new. He nearly turned into an icicle last year because he had some leaky waders. The overalls were water-proof, and even if there was a small leak, at least his legs would stay warm. He slipped into some loafers and went for his first hot cup of coffee. He mused that hunters fifty thousand years ago probably didn't start their day with hot tea or hot coffee. But who knows? Once the Chinese, or whoever it was, discovered the hot morning beverage, they stayed with a good thing. Cleaned out all the pipes in the head. Adam couldn't figure out what use sinuses ever had. Maybe Stone Age hunters had some use for them; maybe they didn't have sinus trouble either.

Adam and Clay had to whisper because Clay's wife was sleeping and intended to keep sleeping. Clay grinned broadly, acknowledging the absurdity of getting up in the cold at this hour. He was tall with a ruddy, Scottish complexion, and still carried himself like the army officer he had been for twenty years before he took early retirement.

"Going to be twenty-five degrees this morning," he remarked.

"We got to be pretty smart characters to go stand in a swamp up to our waists. With that kind of brains, I think we better get some government work."

"It'll build character. At least that's what my old first sergeant used to tell the men."

"I've got about all the character I can stand."

They got their shotguns and shell bags, and each stuck a sandwich in his heavy, camouflaged coat. Outside, Clay's Labrador whined and jumped to the top of the fence. "Not today old podnuh," he replied. The water would be too deep, and they were going to have to wade in. The dog, "Beau," nicknamed for General Beauregard, was beside himself when he was not put in the truck.

The night before, the two men loaded what decoys they could stuff into large net bags they would have to carry into the woods with them. Also their waders and coats. Adam was hoping not to be baptised with swamp water this time out. Clay packed his pipe and lit it, and they started on the hour's drive to Belle Slough. Neither man spoke much, and it was then Adam turned his mind to last night's phone call from his wife. She opened quickly with, "I've got some bad news."

"OK. Let's have it." She knew he didn't like to have anything else said right then except the bare, bad news.

"Rutledge died. Of a heart attack. They're going to bring him back home for burial. The funeral's day after tomorrow."

This meant Adam could hunt only one day, then drive for six hours and still make the funeral. The call came after he and Clay relaxed before the fireplace with some bourbon and ice and commenced to remembering past hunts, especially funny parts when they got stuck, or wet, or something worse. Such moments were becoming more and more important to both of them.

Adam was surprised and a little bewildered, but Rutledge's dying hadn't sunk in. He knew it had happened, but it was more like *knowing* something from television. Not a real knowing, but as if he had been *made aware* of something. Now, though, as he and Clay drove silently through the dark morning toward Belle Slough, Adam realized he had thought about Rutledge in his sleep.

Adam was one of the rare ones who had not had anyone close to him die. Even his parents were still living. His wife, on the contrary, had lost most of her family. Having Rutledge die was a strange experience. He and Rutledge had gone to school together, kept in touch. Sometimes his friend was on the other side of the world, but still they exchanged the occasional letter. Rutledge was a writer who made his living in magazine journalism. He had a staccato, hard-hitting style that sold well, especially adapted to writing about war. The violence attracted him, Adam thought, but he would deny that it did. He insisted it was just a way to make a living while he saved money to write his serious stuff. He was thinking about novels, but he was also a poet. He had the good sense to know he couldn't make a living writing poetry. For the last two years he covered one of the interminable Middle East wars, hoping to stick out a long hitch and return with enough loot. Now he was dead.

Belle Slough was a hardwood bottom that stayed mainly dry during the year and then was deliberately flooded just before duck season so the birds would come in to eat the rich acorn crop. It was a popular hunting area and close enough to large towns that hunters could come out. What this meant was, to get away from all the other guns, locals had to wade deeply into the flooded timber. Clay and some others had reconnoitered the good spots before the season started and most of the time could find them in the dark.

A few cars were already at the jumping off point when Adam and Clay drove up. Stepping out of the warm truck was a shock, but the crisp air was invigorating. Two of the men were newcomers and were introduced to the others. Anybody who was invited was vouched for by one of the regulars. One year a guest peppered another hunter with shot as he tried to finish off a wounded duck trying to get away. Somehow that was more than an accident; it was obscene. After the initial confusion and excuses, no one talked for the rest of the hunt. A great embarrassment.

There was not much time for talk this morning as Clay and Adam slipped on their boot liners, then struggled clumsily into the long chest waders. Each helped the other put a big bag of decoys on his back and they were ready to go. Even in the sharp cold, Adam worked up a sweat before they got to the water's edge. Most of his body heat was trapped in the waders and heavy coat.

Single file, they stepped off into the black water. The leader had a small light, and the rest tried to avoid the sunken

21

limbs and stumps or sudden potholes. Last year one of the group fell into the cold water on the way in. His waders filled up and he had to trudge freezing back to the car.

Finally they came to a space ringed with oaks and began to spread the decoys. Groups of drake and hen mallards with a few wood ducks on the outer edges. The wind blew from the west and the floating decoys nearly all faced into it. The ducks would fly in from the east to land, into the wind, so each hunter found a tree he could stand next to from where he could see the incoming birds. Adam loaded his twelve gauge with No. 4s and then leaned against his tree. He broke away the ice ringing the trunk at water level.

Rutledge was still on his mind. They had hunted together once, years back, but the hunt had not been good. Rutledge came dressed for the hunt in a Confederate cavalry hat with a large yellow plume, a great brass CSA buckle on his belt, and smoking a long slender cigar. Some of the other dove hunters looked on amazed. For someone who talked a lot about guns and killing, Rutledge did not shoot well. He made the mistake of drinking before he took to the dove field, and that was just enough to make him miss. Still, when he wrote about it, the hunt turned out beautifully, he had shot well, and he transformed the whole day into a good time.

Adam chided him about the difference between real life and his story, said that there were those who could do and those who could write about it. Rutledge just smiled.

Now Rutledge was gone. His *goneness* surprised Adam, but also he was surprised how the proximity of death, any death, had been kept out of mind for such a long time. He remembered the story in the Bhagavad-Gita, where the god Dharma, in the figure of a crane, asks which of all the world's wonders is the most wonderful, and the answer had been that no man, though he sees others dying all around him, believes he himself will die. Adam extended this even to the ones around him. He remembered having two young dogs, litter mates, that spent their puppy days wrestling and chasing each other until one day a car killed one. For an hour the other dog stayed close by, nudging his brother to begin play again, clearly at a loss. Adam felt like the puppy that had been left.

Just the faintest light showed itself, and he could see most of his fellow hunters outlined against their trees. Slowly the circle of water became a mirror in the increasing light. Taking pictures had forced Adam to remove himself from what was happening in order to plan his shots. It had become a habit, this standing off from things. He imagined photographing this circle of men around the undulating, watery mirror. He would have to be high up for the scene to mean anything to a stranger. Even then, what would it mean unless the viewers had some intimate knowledge of hunters, of their minds. Unless they participated.

Inevitably Adam felt Rutledge's death instructing him. Both men had a wide streak of futurism in them, planning what they were going to do years ahead. Adam felt this was more becoming in undergraduates, but knew it to be an affliction. Planning to be happy. So much of this future never happened.

There was old Rutledge slated for the black hole, where there was no time, no future, no present. Funny about time and space. In space one could reverse direction. He could, and would, wade back through flooded woods to the truck, then to Calloway's, to his small-town law practice and good wife. But time went only one way, and Rutledge had fallen off its arrow. Now the money he saved and the time he saved up for had no meaning.

Unless he hunted, Adam was seldom up at sunrise; the light on the water and against the limbs and trunks of the winter oaks took his breath away. What a beautiful earth! This beauty seemed to be hidden by so many things: filing briefs, searching vendor and vendee records in the courthouse, taking the car to be fixed, going to the dentist, the indoorness of modern life, the general paving of country with highways, shopping malls, parking lots. We have cut ourselves off from the sun and stars. Now we send our proxies to the moon, and maybe in a couple of years to Mars. Beyond the surfaces of the earth the heavens are conveyed to us on the television screen. A proxy vision.

Just then the leader of the procession through the dark broke the silence with his hailing call for mallards. He had seen some greenheads zipping along above the tree tops and was trying to turn them. Immediately Calloway broke in with his beseeching hail. This was one of the best parts of duck hunting, Adam thought. Talking to the animals. To know the language of animals is a magic, a way of passing through an inscrutable barrier, a way to get beyond the surfaces to some deep down thing. Both men began the clucking of feeding ducks, trying to draw the circling birds to them.

Adam lost sight of the ducks because he kept his face down so as not to be seen, showing only the camouflage of his hat. They would shy away if they saw an upturned face. "Here they come," the closest hunter whispered, and from the east they were dropping through the trees, wings flared for landing when the farthest shooter opened up and a single drake dropped to the water while the others beat frantically for height. Adam's heart raced as the others managed to escape. Such an ecstacy! The mallards, the oak, the hunters, all one brilliant convergence of design!

While the successful hunter waded for his duck, the others resumed the vigil by their oaks. Everyone was much more alert now since this first eruption out of the breaking dark. What if life could be like such peaks, Adam thought. Instead, there were great stretches of silence punctuated by swift pleasure . . . and pain. And death. Rutledge's. His very life had been a swift inflorescence, like a solar flare the recent pictures of the sun revealed. Like it, no one knew when the apogee would occur. Like the sudden appearance of the mallards, Rutledge emerged out of the mystery, then returned to it. Each scene leaving one death. Both appearances concentrated time into nodes of beauty before the falling away.

For a moment Belle Slough became the Slough of Despond for Adam, but he jerked himself back to the present. Deep in the woods he heard the rising whistle of a wood duck. Clay picked out his one wood-duck call from his lanyard and whistled back. Again, the shaman magic of talking to the unseen birds. Adam promised himself again to practice his calling during the off-season. Since he was not skilled, he deferred to the initiated.

Suddenly their circle of hunters seemed to be a spiraling vortex for all the wood ducks in Belle Slough. "Two hens at ten o clock!" Clay yelled, both he and Adam catching the two hens in the midst of oak limbs and stunted trees. Again the racing of the heart as the birds plummeted to earth. Adam waded out and picked up his first of the day. As he returned to his tree, he realized he had forgotten a bag to put his kills in. He dropped the hen between himself and the trunk of the tree, hoping it would float there, but spent the rest of the hunt keeping his kills from drifting away in the slow, imperceptible current.

Almost immediately there was shooting to their right and left, and the woods were alive with ducks. Even though four or five hunters fired, still the wood ducks came, as if willingly meeting the hunters. They were used to feeding on the acorns every morning at this spot, and they were going to come, hunters or not. Like humans, Adam thought, they changed their behavior only under the whip of necessity.

There was a danger now that someone would follow the flight of a duck through the labyrinth of limbs and finally swing his shotgun on line with another hunter. Just as it was difficult to follow two rabbits at once, it was difficult to keep one eye on a flying wood duck and one out for eight other hunters. Now and then someone yelled, "I'm over here, over here!" to warn the busy shooter.

The daily limit had been changed again this year and some were still confused about the law. The limit was three ducks, but no more than two hens. Adam knew his third duck had to be a drake, and consequently he had to shoot with great control. A pair came speeding through the trees to Clay's left, and he snapped off a shot, watched his final bird hit the water. His shot marked a lull in the shooting. The men began to talk quietly, everyone relaxed with the good luck.

"It's a hard job," grinned Clay, "but someone has to do it."

"You're right," Adam agreed. "Laboring over a hot shotgun all day."

Soon there was quiet again. The wind stopped and the pool they stood in was unruffled, now mirroring everything above it. Even the floor of the swamp was visible, leaves and stumps standing out clearly in the bright morning sun. The crowded sounds of early morning frogs and insects, of crows and a hundred perching birds, subsided. Clay twice blew the mournful whistle of the wood duck. Adam concentrated on the woods behind him.

Then the shirring wings of a drake whipped in from the right, and with a smooth, unthinking movement, Adam pointed. Just then the drake passed through a bright shaft of light, and all the reds, blacks, and greens seemed to catch fire, to show forth some unleashed divinity in a forest epiphany. In a great coalescence, the bird and Adam became one. And he tumbled from the air.

"That winds it up." Clay said as Adam waded through the oaks to retrieve the fallen duck.

He picked up the bird carefully, examining the almost carved lines of color. "Well, old fellow, you make the limit," said Adam.

Clay loaned him a piece of cord to tie his ducks together. He then tied the cord to his belt and the three ducks floated behind as he helped to pick up the decoys and stuff them into the net bags. Everyone was talking happily as the men waded for the decoys. Numerous hunts during the last several years had passed with no shooting at all. Fewer ducks were coming from the north because the thousands of potholes and small pieces of wetlands had been plowed under.

Adam was beginning to feel like a dinosaur. The world had changed so fast that he and his ways were going to be extinct soon. He had a feeling of helplessness mixed with anger. Was the whole world going to be turned into the slums of New York and Calcutta? Sometimes Adam felt many humans must have a tremendous resentment against nature, like hating your mother and father, intent on blotting out the memory of the source. That somehow their birth hadn't been tidy, tidy like their city apartments. A fastidious urban puritanism. Like life was only an idea.

Finally all the decoys were packed. Soon the men were wading single file back through trackless water. The walking, or trudging, was not as difficult as it had been in the dark, but still there was the sudden hole to watch for. Adam was at the end of the procession, sometimes falling behind as he went back in time, remembering Rutledge, flying ducks, and many things that had been and were no more.

Long before there were large cities, Anaximander wrote that it was necessary for things to perish into that from which they were born, for they paid one another penalty for their injustice according to the ordinance of Time. This had puzzled Adam when he first read it. Now he thought the old Milesian was expressing the way, the *tao*, that darkness becomes light, and then the return to darkness, the ascendancy of birth and growth and the falling away. In the flux of things, there was that which gathered itself into being, now a flower, now a duck, a poet. This gathering reached its limit, then fell away into the limit of death. Perhaps the way small waves make their procession and flash beautiful with the light, then descend to the formless water of the fecund swamp.

The attempts to deny these limits, which Adam found rampant nowadays, filled him with dread and even disgust. The limit on ducks was a meager one, but a necessity. Clay and he both knew hunters who killed whatever flew in front of them, missing a great point. They were no different in kind from the big-time urban marauders and poachers. Devil take the hindmost.

Ritual, even etiquette, seemed to have disappeared in Adam's lifetime. What was left was naked appetite, unbound to any necessity. Adam had the eerie realization that he was part of a dying civilization and, with the speed of current events, the end would not be long in coming. Well, he must do what he could, but he felt pessimistic for his children, just beginning their adult lives.

At last the men emerged from the water and shadowy swamp. After their legs had pushed against water for so long, they suddenly felt the change of bounding into a lighter medium. Like the speeded up transition of a sea creature adapting to land.

Back on the road, they were happy to divest themselves of their load of decoys, their game and guns. Then to emerge from their chrysalis of waders and heavy coats. Back to normal. They stood around briefly re-telling some of their shots, laughing at their misses, then shook hands all around.

Back home, after giving Beau a pat on the head, they took their six ducks to the back yard. Clay had made a bench out of some thick planks and left it under a big tree. He cleaned his fish there in the summer, his game in winter.

"Let's breast most of them. Maybe just keep the mallard whole," Clay said. He cut an incision down the middle of the breast just under the skin line. Adam held the skin apart while Clay cut gently down the breast bone, then under the breast. From each duck there were two thick red pieces. The feathers and carcasses were in a bag nearby.

"Something to remember the hunt by," grinned Adam, taking one of the prettiest feathers from a male wood duck. He stuck it in his hat.

Soon there was a rosy pile of meat on the bench top. Plucking the mallard was a longer task, but when they finished, the bird lay intact. Three of the shot pellets had left dark marks across the breast, like stigmata. Both men washed their hands and rinsed the pieces of meat.

"Let's get these breasts in some oil and a little wine. I normally like to soak them for twenty-four hours, but since you'll be pulling out in the morning, we'll do the best we can."

Right, thought Adam. Got to bury Rutledge tomorrow. Wonder where he's lying right now? Closed up in a box in an unfamiliar room.

Carol, Clay's wife, had left a note that she was shopping. After Clay mixed the marinade for the breasts, he said, "I don't know about you, but I could stand a shower and a little snooze."

"Sounds good," agreed Adam. Later, on his bed, he reflected how abruptly death had taken his friend, how unnatural it seemed. There's always that problem, trying to explain suffering and death. He doubted he would ever get it right. What to do in the meantime? Whatever the reason, this was the only world he and Rutledge had: imperfect, unpredictable. But there would be no journey, nothing to do, if all of it was perfect and predictable. Guess you have to do with life what Rutledge did with his story of the good hunt where he shot well. Transform it. Take the gold from the ore. And show your panache. Why not? He smiled as he remembered his friend firing away at the incoming doves, the feathers in his cavalry hat waving audaciously in the breeze. Adam knew he better start paying attention. With this he fell into sleep.

He was awakened by the delicious smell of baking bread. After dashing some cold water in his face, he found Clay in the kitchen with Carol. "The old girl decided to bake in your honor," smiled Clay.

"I figured the mighty hunters would be starving," she said. Clay began retrieving the breasts from the marinade.

"Let me help," Adam said. He felt a need to be a part of the cooking. Not just a spectator. He wound each half breast in strips of bacon. The bacon fat, he knew, would help baste the lean meat of the breast. The breasts were thick muscle from the rapidly moving wings, dark red because of the need for large amounts of blood.

Soon the breasts were over the coals in the smoker. "They don't take very long," said Clay. "A fellow cooked them like this for the Ducks Unlimited supper last year. He stole the show."

The sun was setting by the time the smoking was finished. As if in a final, triumphant gesture, the sun's rays struck the underside of a line of clouds, bathing the world in its rosy light. At the table the three of them raised their glasses of burgundy in toast. "Here's to next year's hunt," offered Clay.

"Here's to right now," rejoined Adam. With each morsel of the dark meat, he thought how beautiful the duck's flight had been and how beautiful the duck was now. How important it was to eat when one was eating.

An Imitation

❧ ❦

It behoveth thee to be a fool for Christ
Thomas à Kempis

Hawkins was doing his version of an Iranian student who had missed eight weeks of class yet wanted an "A" in the calculus course.

"I know you are vondering why I have not to come to class since school start. I am good student. You can tell. But I am only support of my wife, my brother, my mother, and now my cousins from Iran. I must work all the time."

"It must be hard. Maybe you ought to drop out. You've missed all the quizzes."

"Oh, I can never do it. I must graduate in three years. Absolutely. I have had calculus in high school. It is very easy for me."

"I understand. But you've never been to class and never taken any quiz. You've got an 'F' as of right now."

"I was really hoping for an 'A.'"

Hawkins' Iranian accent was perfect, and the people at the party howled with laughter. His face could change radically and with great rapidity. One moment he could be Mussolini, posturing before his troops, the next a ghetto kid playing basketball. He became these people. While he was an undergraduate he had done standup comedy in small nightclubs. After his own schooling was completed, he taught mathematics at the University of Houston, and now he was teaching math at the medical school.

He was envied and admired by the young, upwardly mobile professionals of his set in Houston. The surgeons made more money, but none of them seemed to have as much fun as Hawkins. Lately, he was envied even more because he enjoyed the freedom that followed the breakup of his marriage. No one said this, but the surgeons and lawyers still had to have their affairs on the run, in secret. Hawkins was having the time of his life right before their very eyes. Or so they thought. He still had his five-year-old 450 SL convertible. His former wife got the house, but he had moved into one of those opulent apartment complexes that try to simulate Caribbean resort hotels. A great plastic dome covered the pool and hot tubs; and the recreational area, the Pleasure Dome, looked like part of the Amazon rain forest airlifted in.

Yet with the jazzy apartment, sports car, and plenty of money from his job, Hawkins lived with a low-frequency anxiety just underneath all that he thought and did. He felt as if his life had no pattern, that it might have been assembled from different suppliers scattered around the country by someone who had never seen a man before.

He left the party with his latest love, a chesty physical therapist who was into cats and computers. She was trying to work out the physics of a new routine to help a male patient stand more upright by lying on his back and doing some new exercises. She had come to Hawkins for help. He helped her into bed.

This night, after the usual frenzy in bed, he lay awake while she dozed. Her giant, tailless Manx cat sat on the nearby chest of drawers and stared at him. He looked as big as a bobcat. Staring. The hard eyes made Hawkins feel like the stranger he was in this bedroom. He finally dozed for a few minutes, only to be awakened by the cat when it lunged on the bed and began pawing Hawkins' foot under the sheet. He kicked the cat off the bed and hurriedly put on his clothes, as he explained to the startled therapist that he needed to get home.

Three days later he came down with rheumatoid gonorrhea. His knees and elbows had swelled, and he began to feel not very upwardly mobile. While he was undergoing treatment, he couldn't drink, and he found himself loading up with ice cream at the nearby Baskin-Robbins. This led him to much solitary introspection. It was while browsing through the Praline Pecans, the Mocha Chocolates, the Paradise Pineapples that he ran into a quiet, brown-eyed woman who also lived in his complex. She lacked the glamorous look that would have made her a natural target for Hawkins. Now, given the judgment that had fallen upon him, given his dark remorse, he was not feeling so glamorous himself. Thus began his relationship with Monica.

Since sex was out of the question, Hawkins began for the first time to talk to a woman with no intention of seducing her. In the evenings after his classes at the medical school he would stroll over to her apartment where she usually busied herself cooking an evening meal. By then she had slipped out of her secretary clothes and into jeans, looking like the East Texas farm girl she was. Her parents had urged her to learn typing, believing it would end up being worth more than the high school diploma, so maybe she wouldn't have to stay on the farm. Frankly, she liked the farm, but her father felt this was a step up.

For Hawkins, who had grown up in Chicago, Monica was as exotic as a Guatemalan Indian. He kidded her ways and speech as she fixed them field peas and cornbread and one weekend her version of East Texas barbecue. The peas had come from her father's garden. Hawkins would do his version of a hick farmer, and Monica would smile and keep on cooking. It came to him that the plainness of the food and even the unadorned healthiness of Monica were just what drew him, what kept him there. She had a strong body and good legs which were more apparent when she was in her jeans. Around her small waist she wore a western belt with a large silver buckle. She carried herself with vitality that was self-restrained, bounded. He carried the painful reminder of the women who hung out in all the clubs full of designer plants and designer pants. A darkness had, in fact, moved in even before the gonorrhea. He was not sure of the cause . . . maybe it was just leaving his wife. When he had found no one else that seemed to suit him, he fell into a state of drift. He drifted among a woman with a cat, a woman with a membership in a tennis club, and a medical student trying to improve her grade.

Late one evening as he sat at poolside, his feet dangling in the water, he heard, "OK, Hawkins, what's this story I hear about you hustling a Christer. I knew you were kinky, but this sounds like reverse kinky."

His wise-cracking friend Barolo backstroked down the pool to where he sat. Barolo had had the typical reaction to Hawkins' misfortune with the gonorrhea. He had laughed. Hawkins was irritated by this, but guessed he would have done the same, though if someone caught the flu nobody laughed in his face. He remembered that in the army everyone howled when someone got the clap. Some applause!

A scholar draftee volunteered that the word "clap" came from Old French, from brothel and venereal sore. Nowadays it looked like the whole city was a brothel.

Barolo heaved himself from the pool, and as he sat next to Hawkins the water streamed down through the hair of his chest and legs. "So what's this taking up with a fanatic?" he cackled.

"I don't have anything else to do. Besides, she's a nice girl. She plays the organ at church. When's the last time you went out with a nice girl?"

"Ha. You'll see to her corruption. Wait'll the church elders get on to you. They'll see you in the stocks and lashed till you bleed."

"I met some of them once. They're not so bad. Most of them are insurance salesmen or real estate brokers."

"Right. A good place to make business contacts. So . . . you've even been hanging out at church."

Just then the resident manager dimmed the lights in the Pleasure Dome. It was eleven o'clock. In the false twilight they continued to talk.

"Yeah, I've been visiting the natives. Monica invited me to go and I don't mind. It's like doing anthropology in some exotic place."

"Watch out you don't go native. It's happened to some anthropologists. They start out with a kind of noblesse oblige and before you know it they've married the chief's daughter or shaman's son and they're there for the duration. They're as misguided as Rousseau, that oaf."

Hawkins knew he could expect an edge on anything Barolo might say about Christians. For Barolo had been one. Born one, raised one. Then he turned away. Not forty-five degrees, but one hundred and eighty. Hawkins had nothing in his experience that was much like that. He grew up believing in baseball. His father had died when Hawkins was still in junior high and he had gone to church with his mother for the funeral. He had been in another church when he got married. That was his wife's idea. She didn't go to church either, but she couldn't have all the show, the bridesmaids, the reception, without doing the whole thing. It was like getting in costume for a school play. Besides, her parents put on a real feed after the ceremony—caviar, champagne, the works. He knew, though, that Barolo, as a matter of principle, wouldn't walk into a church. Give him a few drinks and he could get fired up and rolling. At a party one night someone rattled his cage and he could be heard above everyone else: "Leap of faith, leap of faith. What they don't tell you is you could just as easily land on Ra the Sun God or Quetzalcoatl! All they really mean is tyranny of the local. It's like a Soviet election. One candidate."

Hawkins smiled to himself as he thought of that evening, and he smiled outwardly now, glad to have this odd, witty companion in a town where he didn't have many friends who could be witty or serious about anything except their latest tennis racquet, their newest restaurant find. What Hawkins found pleasing was the serious way he was funny, the serious world he was laughing about, his slanted wit slipping through the world in ways most people never imagine. While the jokes sometimes were tinged with a slight bitterness, it was from the kind of integrity one expected in mathematics, but was much harder to maintain in the world outside of numbers. The world of contingency outside of numbers was one where a husband and wife could betray each other, the domain of gonorrheas.

Somehow to become one with his friend's mind, Hawkins began to talk in the accents of a Protestant TV preacher, as if he were offering a gift to Barolo for his company. "We are gathered together tooodaaay here in Gawwwd's House to give thanks for living in this gret country of ours. Let us remember our fighting men who guard our freeedooms as we approach this Easter season." Soon Barolo was grinning, relishing a guy from Chicago who had the ear for East Texas or, better, Big Thicket Protestant.

"I got to watch you religious types," he said. "You've commercialized Easter with chocolate rabbits and chicken eggs. Soon you'll be turning to my one big American holdout, Thanksgiving. Porcelain gift turkeys that lay candy eggs or else eight red-nosed turkeys, 'On Hobble, On Gobble,' will be flying down my chimney demanding my damn credit card before they'll leave anything."

"Gawwwd giveth or taketh away, but no credit," rejoined Hawkins.

One day late in February, a false spring day but full of promise, Monica invited Hawkins out to a Big Thicket dinner at the family farm. Her home was not some sprawling ranch house, but a clean, well-kept frame house with big porches front and back. The barns were close by, with an ample garden space, now mostly containing the remains of winter vegetables like turnips and collards, separating them from the house. His northern accent drove home that he was a stranger, but he was Monica's friend, so he was taken right in by the weather-lined father and the tanned, plump mother, and by Monica's two rowdy teenage brothers. Straightaway the brothers had him out at one of the barns looking at their cutting horses; both brothers were wearing hats as big as umbrellas, their jeans, belts, and boots following a dress code as rigid as a Marine guard's.

At midday dinner the table top was jammed with food, with lots more on a sideboard. A big hen with cornbread dressing occupied the center, but fanned out below this mountain of glazed tawniness were great foothills of field peas, potato salad, and a huge round of cornbread flanked by a barbecued ham with links of pork sausage around it, a giant white boat of gravy, a hummock of rice, and a quivering mound of cranberry jelly looking nervous before what was to come. Monica's father asked God to bless all this opulence, thanking Him at the same time for their guest, and even though Hawkins felt self-conscious being singled out for God's notice, he felt like he had been made welcome.

Halting long enough to give God his due, Monica's rambunctious brothers put on an eating display that would have stirred the envy of Aga Khan. Hawkins generally had salad at most for lunch and even before the apple pie and ice cream arrived he was reeling. Fortunately, nothing was expected of him after this ritual feast except to sip strong coffee in a rocking chair on the front porch while the brothers put on a riding display in the front yard. How they managed it so soon after dinner Hawkins could not imagine.

On the long drive back to Houston, facing a setting sun, he felt how important such gatherings had become, especially now. This family's daughter had gone off to the jungle of Houston to make her solitary way, far from the vortex of the family, partly because her father felt she would be better off there. No doubt because he felt the labor wouldn't be as hard. Hawkins wondered how good the trade had been, swapping harder work for the loneliness of the city. He felt that he was losing his trust in progress.

As he recalled the parting scene with Monica's family in the yard, watching them leave for the city, it seemed like a classical frieze on some temple, or an old photograph from an earlier time in America, the weathered couple in plain dress, as if they had been together from the beginning of time, and their offering to time to come in their cowboy sons astride their mounts, ready to shoot it out with Death if he had dared to show his face. How had he, Hawkins, smart guy from Chicago, failed to figure out the right moves? He had been fast on his feet. What had been missing?

His Mercedes sports coupe swept into a darkening Houston. The outskirts were filled with drilling equipment sitting idle from an oil boom gone bust. Row upon row of thrown-up apartment complexes were vacant or abandoned. A dying city. Near the interstate highway, from the broken window of an abandoned house, a curtain blew outside as if to wave goodbye.

Monica's church decided to put on a play, to be performed the week before Easter. At supper one evening she shyly asked him if he would be in it. Since there would be so many male parts—to start with, twelve disciples plus Jesus—they were running short of grown men in their twenties and thirties. Hawkins was momentarily at a loss, but then he began to think what a funny idea that was, him playing one of the disciples.

The next evening the two of them went to the big room in the "education" center near the main church building where there were many small classrooms and one central hall with a raised platform. When necessary, this could be turned into a makeshift stage, but the actual performance would be in the church auditorium.

After a little milling around, the youth director, a bald yet youngish-looking man, called out in a prissy way for them to gather round. "A good group, a good group. We're going to have lots of fun and we're going to put on a really good show." He swelled with self-importance. One might have thought he was directing a Hollywood cast of thousands rather than the few who would carry out the intimate drama of the last night before the crucifixion.

All but Hawkins were known to the director, although he had seen him once on an earlier Sunday when he had come with Monica. The roles of ten disciples were promptly handed out to the men best known to the director, and for the first time Hawkins learned that there were two Simons, Simon Peter and Simon the Zealot. Most of the others had not known it either. Hawkins discovered that there had been two Judases, too! And Judas, the son of James, was given to the other remaining actor.

"Oh, dear, I do hope you won't mind playing Judas Iscariot," fluttered the director, looking at Hawkins.

Monica laughed, uneasily. "I didn't prepare him for something like this."

"It's OK, it's OK. It's only a play," Hawkins said.

"Well, I guess that leaves me to play Jesus," the director said, resigned. "So. A word about the costumes. We won't wear our modern clothes, but since we don't have wigs available, we'll just have to do without. Anyone wanting to grow a beard, or borrow one, that's fine." He handed out the typed scripts. "Let's just run through it once tonight so you'll know what to expect. You can learn your lines at home."

Hawkins followed the plot with great interest. He knew generally how things went, but none of the specifics. Like the two Simons and two Judases. The cast practiced breaking invisible bread and drinking invisible wine from a common cup. Hawkins thought he might have the best part. Simon Peter was a pretty good one, too.

Judas could have come straight out of a Chicago Mafia movie, Hawkins thought. He goes over to another family, the chief priests and scribes, and cuts a deal to set up his own godfather. They tell him when they want it, not on a holiday (bad press). Judas goes back to his own family, and as he drinks wine with his godfather, the godfather looks him right in the eye and hints that he knows something is going down. One of the troubles Hawkins had staying in the mood of his part was the prissy, balding Jesus.

Still, Hawkins was interested in his own part. It always seemed like bad guys in the movies—in life for that matter—had been more interesting. Like bad women. Hard to explain.

For the next week he thought a lot about Judas. Even though the little play had the same plot year after year with no revisions, he figured it was a good idea to read up on it. One of the confusing aspects of the story, and the parts played by Judas and Peter, was Jesus telling them what they were going to do before they did it, kind of giving away the end. But then everybody knew the end of the play anyway. At first his notion was that knowing the end made it unrealistic. But as he pondered over this and Judas' betrayal, it came to him that the plot of everybody's life was rather similar if you took the high points: birth, growth, and death. Everyone knew the ending, just like Jesus's. It was just not knowing the timing. About all one could do was consider the style that would be his own. Judas no doubt considered himself a flexible kind of guy, one who could change grounds pretty quick, looking out for the main chance. It wasn't like the town hadn't thought he was doing a useful thing. He was going to get himself a little piece of land with the money, sort of God's little acre, Hawkins laughed. Starting over.

Hawkins thought he was slowly getting into Judas' head. It took a lot of individuality to do what Judas did. Like some sort of Cold War spy who had to operate mostly alone, be his own man.

All went smoothly until the youth director ended up in the hospital. It was discovered he had a hole in his heart and would have to have an operation. Hawkins got this news from Monica one evening, and she seemed much flustered about what would happen to the play. She talked to the minister, and he said perhaps he could fill in with the directing chores, but that he didn't feel he ought to be playing Jesus. It ought to be someone from the congregation. When Monica had approached a fellow from the Young Adult Sunday School class, he said he didn't want to play Jesus either, but he would play one of the disciples if he was hard

41

pressed. Hawkins saw it coming, like a slow curve headed to third base, then turning straight for where he stood.

"Who? Me?"

"We're really in a jam, and I don't know who else can save us." Monica's big, brown Texas eyes pleaded with him. When his friend Barolo dropped by again, he howled.

"I warned you about going native, didn't I? I have to admit even I didn't think you would go this far."

"I knew you'd take it well," Hawkins grinned.

"I thought this was just a way to stay around your new chick, but I think you're caught. Just think of all that good scientific education going down the tubes."

"That doesn't have anything to do with it. I'm just helping these people out. Maybe they recognize good acting talent."

"Hollywood couldn't get big-name actors to play that spectacle about Jesus several years ago. Had to get an unknown. There's a danger in starting at the top. Kind of hard for people to take an actor seriously playing one of the Three Stooges once they've seen him play God."

"Only half God."

"Listen to the new theologian. Tell me, old buddy, how do you square all this magic with yourself?"

"I'm just scouting the scene out, trying to see what all the fuss is about. Doing a little archaeology. Can't hurt anything. Besides, I still get Monica," he grinned, raising his eyebrows like Groucho Marx and tapping his imaginary cigar.

"Just a little empirical reconnaissance, huh? Trying to get a little certainty, is that it? You'd be better off doing your science if certainty's what you hunger for."

"That's getting to be a laugh and you know it. You should have learned from your boys Poincaré and Göedel that science rests on assumptions like everything else. These assumptions are just convenient, just conventional. Of course, we can't go around telling the uninitiated that. They'd find out what charlatans we are."

"So you're ready to substitute the blood of the Lamb for the axioms of mathematics, is that it? You're a queer one, Hawkins. I think the clap has gone to your head."

"We'll see. Who knows, I may be launching an acting career."

"Or we might commit you soon to the loony bin. This clap must have really scared you."

The closer Hawkins drew to the actual performance, the more the part of Jesus occupied his thoughts. He was not used to doing serious parts. Irony, cracking wise, impersonation had been his strong suit. Besides, he hadn't had any professional training. In college he had practiced with a buddy for their comic routines. His timing was meshed with the other's response. He could give tips to his partner and vice versa. A hand gesture, a drooping clown's mouth of sadness, a double take. But here he was alone.

Part of Hawkins' difficulty was getting into the head of his character. Judas had been a lot easier. He just put himself in the place of the Mafia stoolie and went from there. But how did you get into the head of God, or half-God, or whatever this mysterious combination was? Soon he was pouring over the conflicting accounts in the gospels in the evening with Monica. Like many who had grown up in the church, Monica knew the general story, but she had a hard time answering the questions Hawkins was asking. For her, the story was not a mental problem, something to be taken apart and looked at in pieces. The story was as much a part of her as the sounds and smells of the church sanctuary, of Easter and Christmas. Hawkins was pursuing this like research at the medical school. He wanted specific details about background. Monica borrowed several Biblical commentaries, and soon Hawkins was over his head in abstruse arguments about the text.

What did Judas actually do? Did he just identify Jesus to

the police or had he given the Sanhedrin inside dope about Jesus' secret claim to be the Messiah? Was the Last Supper a day before the Passover? Hawkins was swamped in minutiae. It happened that way in his school research sometimes. He had to back off and try to remember where he really wanted to go.

He focussed on this group as Oriental men who had been together through hard times and who were meeting to break bread in an upstairs room. This tight circle would break apart within hours. Hawkins tried to think of instances of betrayal in his own life. Like when his wife and he betrayed each other but nothing was said, nothing was acknowledged. Jesus knew that Judas was going to turn stoolie on him and that his good friend Simon Peter would take a walk when they accused him of being a friend of Jesus. Hawkins began practicing his face, a face that would carry all the sadness in his eyes.

Besides that, Hawkins concentrated on the garden scene. During the day, Jesus had been preaching in town, but at the end of each day he liked to get away from the noise and crowds to a place on nearby Mount of Olives, a small garden called Gethsemane. After supper on this last night, he did the same, and it caught Hawkins' attention that he anticipated what was going to happen back in town, that he was torn between what he might have to do, and the hope that there was some other way. That he was not sure. There was real anxiety here. Hawkins could get into that. Jesus dreaded going ahead, because he was not absolutely certain that this was what he needed to do.

Monica had in the meantime made her version of what a Palestinian would have worn during the time of the play. One evening she had asked Hawkins to let her pin the cutout material on him in order to get the right fit. As she moved around him tucking here, pinning there, he began to be aroused as she touched him. He forced himself to think of something outside Monica's room, which was becoming close, even warm. He focussed on the red hibiscus he could see out Monica's window that faced the gardens of the Pleasure Dome. With his attention on the red flower, he felt warmth move up from the base of his spine and travel to his neck, suffusing him alternately with small chills and a delicate feverishness. He needed to get back to his own apartment.

Later in the week, he slipped on the finished costume of rough cotton muslin, dyed a deep maroon, in his own living room. He had grown a short beard that fitted the traditional version. Fate would have it that Barolo came strolling into the apartment when Hawkins still had the robe on. For a moment, Barolo thought he was in the wrong apartment, or that he had come upon something very private, but once his common sense returned, he gasped with laughter. Hawkins was embarrassed, but he knew he had to let the laughter run its course.

Soon the week before Easter came. Hawkins was surprised how fully this play had taken over his time, how he now focussed on this above all things day and night. When the disciples gathered for the dress rehearsal, he noticed how having all the men dressed in the old way caused the whole action to take on more power.

Another change had been more subtle. Since the minister was merely filling in for the director and had no pretensions about his theatrical calling, the actors had to work matters out themselves. Gradually, Hawkins came to guide their gestures and speeches. Being Jesus had something to do with it, since he was the main player, but because Hawkins had been reading all the Bible commentaries, he filled in a lot of background and at the same time lent a sense of freshness, even urgency, to how they were to play their parts, how the play was to go.

The big night came, and the large sanctuary was filled. For Hawkins, by this time, all the murmuring people became the citizens of Jerusalem just before Passover. The front of the sanctuary had been completely darkened, and when the lights came on the disciples were in their places for the scene of the Last Supper. There were soft "ooohs" and "aahs" from the audience. Then the scene settled down to the dialogue between disciples and to questions addressed to Jesus. Finally Hawkins rose and broke the bread for those at the table, telling them that he very much wanted to eat the bread with them but would not eat again until the kingdom of his father had come. The same with the goblet of wine. "Pass this among you and drink, but I will not drink until my father's kingdom comes."

After this, Hawkins dropped the bombshell: "The hand of one of you who will betray me is on this table." The latecomer who had taken the part of Judas looked down like a scolded dog. "Woe unto the man who betrays me." After this moment, the discussion turned to who was going to be boss after Jesus left the scene, and one or two of the disciples managed to get a laugh from the audience as they fussed and preened about their relative importance in the group. The scene turned serious again when Simon Peter insisted that he was going to prison with Jesus if necessary, this after Jesus had told him Satan was after him. The little scene closed with Jesus telling Peter that three times before the cock crowed again he was going to deny even knowing him.

The second scene was still in the upstairs room and largely of Jesus going over their year together, all the hard times and the good times. How, even though they had no money or even shoes, they had stuck together and their faith had sustained them. Now the testing would begin again in earnest. He was to be tested; so were they, for all his work was left up to them and he was counting on them. As Hawkins spoke, he felt a sadness. They would betray Jesus, he had betrayed his wife, the girl with the cat had betrayed him.

The last scene of this short play was set in the garden. The disciples were all on the left side of the stage and Hawkins on the far right. The potted palms gave a good semblance of a garden as Hawkins knelt to pray with his body facing forty-five degrees to the audience. Most of the stage was dimmed, with a soft spot on Hawkins as he began speaking quietly to his Father, asking Him if he wanted to change His mind about what seemed headlong and inevitable. That maybe what would serve best would be to go back to the countryside and continue to preach.

Hawkins remained quiet for a moment, and then a shudder passed through him. His whole countenance changed, as the skin drew tightly across his facial bones, and the perspiration broke out on his forehead.

The silence in the sanctuary deepened, as if a vast abyss had appeared. The people in the audience were rapt, embraced as they were by the dark security of their vantage point and the intimate vulnerability they were privy to. Monica played the organ softly to close the scene.

Had this drama been elsewhere the audience could have released the tension with applause. Instead they flocked around Hawkins when the play was over. His face still glistened with perspiration and he seemed exhausted. Members of the congregation said several times what a natural actor he was. He smiled a little, but seemed like he was somewhere else, even disoriented.

Monica came from her place at the organ. Standing back at the edge of the admirers, she frowned slightly, looked worried. When the others moved away she asked anxiously, "Are you OK?"

"Yes," coming back from where he had been. "Yes. I believe so."

As Hawkins left the sanctuary and walked with Monica out into the night and under the distant stars, he passed from one shock to another. From the closeness of the sanctuary he emerged through its doors into a vast emptiness, an emptiness that contained Houston, Palestine, and Alpha Centauri and sped away into inconceivable darkness. Yet, for all its greatness, it was the immense void he had taken into himself moments before in the sanctuary that left him drained. Empty, he walked on through the night with Monica, knowing that he was now required to keep this emptiness pure, like a bowl that waited to be filled.

The Commuters

❧ ❧

The car was due any minute. I try to keep an eye out, get some coffee in me, and stuff my books and papers into a briefcase. Our trip takes an hour from my place, which is on the semi-rural outskirts of the city. It takes Simone and Staunton twenty minutes to get to me. We teach at a small bush-league college in Blackston, Louisiana. Simone is a post-war immigrant from France who teaches French. Staunton is a post-war homosexual (species, discreet) who teaches Spanish and does so because that was the easiest language he could get into. I am the youngest of the commuters, but none of us has finished our doctoral work which is the only reason we travel to Blackston. Blackston College takes what it can get.

The 1962 Chevrolet swirls into my driveway at seven-thirty. We have been commuting together since last school year and are thus relieved of the necessity of greeting or making first-meeting talk. I get in the back seat and have it all to myself. Staunton is driving, but it is not his car. It is Simone's car, the car her husband had bought new before he died last year. He was Simone's second husband, a full professor at the university in Baton Rouge. I knew him only slightly, but he had seemed a quiet fellow and little match for Simone. It was not Simone that killed him, though, but a peculiar cancer—the kind where you're here today and gone tomorrow with not much visible change or pain in the going. Simone had not seemed very saddened by his death, which was a month or so after we began traveling together.

I found Simone to be an interesting bird, even though she can drive you up the wall in a minute. She has fairly short, curly hair which is black as a raven's wing, and I think the color is natural even though she is in her forties. It's shiny and healthy like a citizen of the Mediterranean. Her eyes are dark brown, but the whites have just a touch of what looks like yellow (more on some days than others) which I suspect derives from her nocturnal imbibing. She brought her love of French wine with her to this side of the Atlantic. We do not socialize together, but she almost daily describes some party she has gone to. She has other features that resemble those of a raven. Her nose has a very high bridge that suggests a beak, and along with her high cheekbones it accentuates her thin, severe face. The face would fit readily in a Goya, but her generally kind and effervescent spirit keeps it from looking like any particular face I have seen in the family of Charles IV, for example. Simone is no devotee of athletics, yet she has a careful, slender figure.

Her greatest misfortune, in my opinion, is her raucous,

screeching voice. I think her classes in French get a very human rendering of certain concierges, however, which must have, for her students, put to rest the cliché that all French is romantic. This is a voice that could momentarily stand against a German infantryman, which it did in 1940, before he belted Simone across her high-bridged nose, slapped her on the rear, and told her to get him something to eat. Her first husband died during the same month, June, when Herr Hitler decided he wanted France, too. One day as we narrowly missed a log truck, Simone told us that her young husband had been run over by one of his own army's trucks. This earned him a French decoration which was given to her.

All in all Simone strikes me as mostly depthless and harmless. One is bound to have some compassion for a woman with two husbands out from under her, in spite of her screeching voice. Staunton has confided rather snigger-ingly that she now and then takes on young men in their twenties. Most of the time this begins with renting them a very cheap room in her big house, or maybe helping them with their French. According to Staunton, they all take advantage—but I think more power to her.

Staunton and Simone are talking about last night's cham-ber ensemble at LSU. They really live in that academic com-munity rather than Blackston's. Of course, Blackston has no chamber ensemble. Most of the faculty who live in Blackston take up hobbies and stack up years toward retirement.

"Did you see how that cellist handled his bow? You would have thought he was cutting up a side of beef," Staunton remarked, keeping his eyes on the road—something Simone had never been able to do. She drove for a week, but we asked her to stop. She kept running off the highway, and this road is not one to be careless on. Two lanes with lots of log trucks.

"Out of all that crowd half of them came to the party

51

afterwards." This remark reflects Simone's real reason for going. She is interested in people.

A great deal of the time Staunton is doing his bitchy best to attack whoever comes within his sights. He is mostly bald at thirty with a few strands of hair pulled over the top and given as much attention as a Medusa at her hairdresser's. He is egg-shaped, but saves himself by wearing very expensive clothes with a conservative style so that he comes off more like a banker. His most distinguishing mark is his missing chin—unusual for someone his age. It is not the result of too much fat; it is just that the bones that should have cantilevered his chin were foreshortened.

"I exchanged a few words with the cellist at the party, and he was perfectly oafish. After the Budapest all this was such a come down." Staunton goes on like this much of the time, and he fits a type so well that after meeting him, most people react the way they do when they see another swallowtail. It's interesting, the swallowtail is behaving quite normally, and they turn their attention to something else. Staunton is just as harmless as Simone, though not as pretty as a swallowtail. And he has to keep up with a lot of names. This coloratura had ousted so-and-so at the Met, this ballet dancer hit his partner with his pump and she *certainly* deserved it, and wasn't it fatefully sad that Gregorian suffered a certain rigidity once it was universally performed in the eleventh century.

After fifteen minutes of the journey, the landscape announces a motif that it would pursue until we get to Blackston. Mostly a poor white version of Fitzgerald's Valley of the Ashes. The land is absolutely flat and the highway closely parallels some railroad tracks. As is not unusual in many sections of the United States, little villages or towns appear with regularity every five miles—towns that had sprung up with the railroad. The first little town was larger than the rest as it was fed by the industry of the city.

Numerous families live here to "get away from it all,"—"all" being the big, bad city.

Passing through this little town today the conversation in our car drops off. Simone fishes around in her purse for some makeup, and Staunton pushes in the car lighter and begins packing a cigarette on the horn. The reason for this nervous silence is that we normally picked up Henry Brown at this point. Even though Henry is not with us now there is still the conditioned reflex to turn down Cloverdale Street and stop in front of his small tract house of dingy pink asbestos siding, the kind of house that looks tempting enough in an architect's rendering but never in reality. It had been run-down when Henry and his wife Audrey rented it. I think the landlord was the Federal Housing Authority because the owner had flown the coop, as Henry used to say. When we would drive up, all of his six children would still be waiting to be taken to school or nursery. His wife occasionally appeared behind the screen door, her hair still up in tight pin curls as she prepared for work. All of their children were under nine years old.

Actually, the Browns were not out of their element in this small town. They had moved down from northern Louisiana, and the people back in the hills there looked like the same breeding that you find here. It's remotely Scotch-Irish but the blood had been tempered in the hot southern sun. Henry's complexion was a brown that was somehow different, though. Everything about Henry was brown, his wavy hair, his eyes, his clothes, his briefcase, as if the artist had been charged with tinting the image to go with his name and life. He was thirty-five years old, but talked like a man fifty or sixty years old in the way that many younger men in the South learn to do.

Henry's avenue to the English Department was not unique; yet, it was still interesting. There are failed preachers, priests, and latter-day mystics in English departments, it seems to me, because this is a refuge of last resort. Many of them had majors in English before they started toward divinity schools. But as their old ghosts deserted them and gradually the places were taken up by others, these people had drifted back into English. We even get some of them over in history where I am. Henry had come from a very poor, red-clay family. As I gather the story, a family in the Baptist church offered to keep him after he was in junior high school and his father had given permission. The school in the hills was not good, and Henry had demonstrated more than the neighborhood average of interest in book things. This all culminated in Henry's graduation from a Baptist seminary, and he and his wife had settled into a par-sonage. I never knew why he left the ministry, but it wasn't because he ceased to have *any* faith, because he still took his family to the Baptist church right up to the end.

After finishing another degree in English, he had joined our group commuting to Blackston. Well, Henry's threshold for ornaments and fluffy art talk was much lower than my own, and since he rode in the back seat with me, we fell to our own conversations most of the time, which bored Simone and Staunton stiff. They certainly didn't feel left out. Henry soon discovered that I was a man of no faith, and of course there is a much more fertile field for discussion between a strong believer and an atheist than between a believer and the nominal believers like Simone and Staunton. Simone was Catholic and Staunton once described himself as very High Church Anglican and one who might bolt for Rome in a fit because of "better theater." His words, not mine.

Henry's "serious conversation" was more his choice than my own. Much of the time such conversations simply lead to flustered feelings with nobody learning anything but having his own position made more intractable. Such matters are one thing over a cup of coffee, but quite another when one is locked into the prison of a commuter's car. Even Simone and Staunton couldn't avoid Henry's talk of salvation and the like. Normally Henry didn't slip off into such cauldrons, and his own faith had eroded enough that he could consider with a renewed curiosity and honesty matters that had fallen into rhythmic affirmation.

Ten or fifteen minutes would often pass with talk about his wife and children. His wife worked as a secretary in the little town and she did not like it. Henry was trying to get enough for a downpayment on a small piece of land where he could garden and have some animals. He thought this would be good for the children, especially, but he said his wife seemed to have little sympathy for this dream, small though it was. Of all places, Henry wanted his land in the vicinity we whizzed past now, hellishly desolate in the winter. In this flat country there were no wild mountains unchanged by the seasons, nor even any snow to cover the dead ocherous land. What broke the dullness were the open sores of greasy-walled filling stations cluttered with piles of old tires and tubes and their ESSO signs that flapped in the February wind.

A subject we had kicked about for several days in the very early fall, I have recalled numerous times in the last two months. Where does one find the imperative for social action if there is no God? Why is he to feel responsible for anyone else? As we turned the matter around and around we naturally got no closer to the answer, I suspect, after the conversations than before. Henry felt (and I must admit my hunch is he was right) that Dostoyevsky's idea that all things were possible if there were no God was the only logical one. It was mostly an accident when I noted one day that one of the new French Existentialists asserted that the basis of responsibility was that one was free to leave the earth if he chose, but that if he decided to stay he was responsible, or that was the gist of it. Henry pondered that, and then we moved on to other matters as the fall came toward us in a shower of lectures and papers to grade. But Henry did not forget the words, for every now and then when some matter at school would come up, perhaps an absurdity that only an administrator could dream up, he would grin one of his rare grins, his white teeth stark against his steady brownness, and remark to me, "Well, if we don't like it we can leave." It was like a private joke that the two of us shared.

Two months ago my back went out as it likes to do in the cold months. All I have to do is twist the wrong way on a cold morning or lift the garbage can wrong and it spasms. I called Simone very early to tell her not to pick me up and at a more respectable time called my department head to let him in on the good news. He is a kindly old man, not given to irony, but on that morning he acknowledged my reason for not coming in as if I were deceiving him. Having the morning face me like it did, I tried to pamper my back. I filled the bath with scalding hot water and turned the radio on, even put a magazine close at hand. The regular five-minute newscast broke the story about a Blackston professor, Henry Brown, who had bludgeoned to death five of his six children, shot his wife, and then blown his own brains out.

The evening paper went into detail, and I called Simone when she returned home, to find out what she knew. Simone declared excitedly that when they got to Henry's house there were police cars all over the place, that nobody was being let in, and that a deputy had simply blurted out, "Ma'am, Mr. Brown ain't going to school this morning. He's done killed himself. Now you'll have to move on, please ma'am." The evening paper said that Henry Brown had the day before gone to a bank in Blackston, borrowed a couple of thousand dollars on his signature, and had the loan insured, which was not unusual. Bankers like to look out for themselves. In the early hours of the morning Henry had called his brother-in-law and told him what he planned to do. The brother-in-law was to pay the funeral expenses with the money he had borrowed and which would not have to be paid back. Before the brother-in-law could call the police and they could get over, Henry had taken a ball-peen hammer and clubbed his big wife first and shot her with a twenty-two pistol either then or later; he then clubbed all of his children with the hammer, and the ones who still moved he shot in the head. Then he killed himself with one shot. There had been some running about, the reporter wrote, because the house was very bloody. The professor had left a note, the story went on, and it said, "This is the only way all of us will get out of this rotten world together." The story concluded that one of the children had survived and was in critical condition.

We don't have far to go now to get to Blackston, and Henry's little town is long gone. Simone and Staunton have resumed their banter about the Metropolitan Opera touring group that will perform "Medea" this coming Saturday. Staunton is comparing this cast with the one he heard at La Scala, or maybe on a record he has.

Henry's action could be understood in a lot of ways, I think. His wife kept harping on him and killing his dreams, he faced frustrating money problems with so many children, and so on. The morning he had gone to the bank he had come by my office to chat, but I was on my way to a class. All I remember was he had a gleam in his brown eyes as if he knew something I didn't know. I only interpret this in this way after the fact. I can't help wondering though, if I had been free to talk with Henry, would it have made any difference. Of course, I can't really be held responsible for something I did not know about.

The people in Blackston have treated the event like scum covering a pond and after a stone is thrown in; the scum

57

covers the hole right back over. It's as if what he did threatened them so much they had to go on the defensive right away. For a lot of the students the explanation was a lot easier because Henry was "in English." If a professor of dairy science had done the same thing it would have been more problematic. I understand the fact that life must go on and that people must turn their attention to the living. There is no reason for the college to stay in mourning for Henry Brown.

I'm the one with a problem, and I know it. Henry is my problem. Why did he do this thing? I remember he used to grind his teeth a lot and the muscles would knot in his jaw. This was the whole time I knew him. So, okay, there was a lot of hostility in him. That doesn't explain it away. And I won't have it, at least in Henry's case, that he was "simply" crazy and didn't know what he was doing. Not that you can't be crazy and lay elaborate plans. Of course you can. But Henry knew what he was about, I am convinced. For those students and teachers who knew Henry, that's what put the mortal fear in them. Which brings up my idle remark about some French Existentialist and what . . . my own culpability? Henry was a grown man. But that does not entirely make his ghost go away. I must say it brought home what bloody instruments ideas are. There is also the problem of why Henry had to kill his children and his wife if he was the one who had decided to go, and this may bear on the whole question.

Henry had no sense of style, and I don't mean this in the flippant way Staunton would have said it. He just had no sense of the right moves. I believe Henry was sincere about killing all his children so that they could go with him. Why he wanted to take his wife leaves me baffled. But then he botched his grand move; he left a daughter with a damaged brain and yet a memory of what had happened. It's a ghastly thought, but he couldn't even do this right.

Matters of style and large ideas should not be pursued

unless one is willing to train for the complete gesture. Otherwise it is as bad as forcing a ten-year-old ballet student to do the *Ritual Fire Dance to Exorcise Evil Spirits*.

We have finished our journey to Blackston, and Simone waves at two of her students. She is well-liked. Which leads me to observe that Simone and Staunton will very likely not murder. I also note that Henry's ghost has not been explained or put to flight. As we get ready to go our separate ways Simone gaily asks me to go to see *Medea* with her on Saturday and to a party afterwards. I surprise her by accepting.

Mr. Bo

❧

His wife had gone in the rickety old Ford to Bayou Goulas to see her old man and her mama and had taken those smart alec kids with her—those goddamn hybrids only a coonass and a redneck could throw. Like a horse and a jenny— throwing a deadend. Some people fancied the old woman might keep the kids and not come back, but it was too much to wish for. And anyway, Bo Simmons was still around. Like rounding up a herd of wild hogs only to find you have left the boar still in the bushes.

He had been on the island in the middle of Tickfaw River all afternoon trying to drive a few cows that always found their way across the river when it was low. But when the hot weather came—and it was hot—the mosquitoes would eat them up. He chose this time because he did not want to have to see the family off. Saying goodbye made him uncomfortable.

The greeting, the salute, that was something else.

It would have been easier to move the cows if he had brought several men. But Bo decided to work alone except for his two Catahoula curs. He had traded for the two dogs in the upper part of the state when they were only puppies. Black and brown patches mottled their white hides. That was striking enough, but it was their eyes caught hold of you—they were ghostly—glass eyes, of a pale, pale blue, almost like an albino's. They were close to the shade of Bo's eyes: startling; you felt Bo could look inside you and know exactly what you were thinking. Well, he must have seen something inside those young puppies. Grown, they had the look of crazies in the asylum. But they knew what Bo wanted when it came to working cows. It was just as well they did.

During the summer the island steamed with heat and moisture. The cypress trees trapped the air and there was little breeze. The cows moved the way they should, and the dogs were in the right places at the right time. This eased the muscles in Bo's stomach and made him forget the weather. The world seemed to function smoother when he was free of people. Not because he could not handle them. Lord knows, he could. But people were fools, the old and the young. Bo had thought it many times. Mainly because they lied to themselves. Not just to other people, which Bo understood. But they were hypocrites before themselves. Fools.

As the last Brahma cow moved to the ford in the river, Bo eased his horse down the steep embankment through a small cut, blocking the way in case one of the cows bolted. As the tall sorrel crossed the narrow strip of sandbar, Bo took his feet from the stirrups and brought his knees high above the saddle, resting his feet on the saddlebow. The swift muddy water rose to the horse's belly, and a good feeling, almost exhilaration, rose up in Bo Simmons, rose from his legs to his head and gave him a shiver. The horse clambered up the dirt bank, and in a few minutes the cattle were shuttled to a nearby pasture. After he got down to close the gap, Bo took off his tattered straw hat and wiped his face and neck with a red handkerchief. The sun had started below the tops of the trees now, and a brief, cool breeze fanned the quietness. Simmons watched the humped, gray cattle move to join the herd in the distance. The sorrel shook his bridle—not a jingle, closer to a rattle. Bo saw a horsefly on the sorrel, crushed it in his hand, and threw it on the ground. He took very good care of his animals. His horse and his dogs gave him the highest, the purest pleasure he was capable of accepting, but he could cut a dog's throat if it did not do what dogs are supposed to do.

The heat had warmed the thousands of honeysuckles to a disconcerting fragrance, and the sudden, cool wind of late evening carried the scent at a time when Bo could think of his own pleasure or think of his own will not so much in conflict with the earth, the weather, or people. He got back into the saddle, the horse still dripping from the ford, picked up the rope reins, and headed down the long lane to his house.

Wagons carrying hay to the barn and sleds with two-by-four runners had worn lines in the mud, and they had been baked there. Simmons rode in the middle of the ruts, his horse clopping along easily. The lane was lined with wild blackberry bushes and this was the time for picking.

As Bo drew close to several small shotgun houses he remembered that he would have no one to cook for him and that he was already hungry. He rode past the first two houses and he was greeted by those sitting on the porch. The hands were in from plowing and were cooling off.

"Howdy, Cap'n." And he would nod.

When he came to the third house, his right eye crinkled a moment in decision, and then he pulled up to the wooden gate.

"Mary!" he hollered. There was no man, no one rocking on the porch at this house. A skillet clanged against a wood stove inside. A woman of maybe forty came onto the porch. She was hefty with strong, thick arms and big hams of hips, thighs, and calves.

"Suh?"

"You might send one of your girls down to cook supper for me. Miz Simmons's gone for a while."

"I kin come down if you want," she answered.

"No. You go on with what you're doing and send one of your girls." He spoke flatly and decisively.

"Yessuh."

Bo clucked to his horse and rode on down the lane. He had allowed Mary to stay on the place even after her husband had one day up and left. It was unusual for Bo to do that because he needed men for the fields, but he had left everything sort of hanging, telling his wife that Mary could help her at the house. He never told Mary flatly that she would be able to stay. This made her feel even more the unsubstantiality of her place, made her a better worker.

When Bo came to the big, dingy farm house, he took his horse to the lot and unsaddled him. He lifted the heavy work saddle with one of his powerful arms and stepped into a room next to the crib. Several ropes dangled from the ceiling, each with a loop at the end. He threaded the one free rope through the hole in the saddlebow and up and over the horn. The room lent itself to fancy in the dusty gloom—the dark-tanned, textured hide of animals, fashioned into something that related to human kind, but hanging static, or swinging gently in the thick, powdery silence.

A thick rat scooted off as Bo stepped heavily on the

wooden floor. Briefly it startled him. He leaned his head out the door and called, "kitty, kitty, kitty." The high, almost falsetto of the call sounded strange, coming from this stern masculine face. A white cat bounded across the lot and stopped silently, anticipatory, with uplifted face, looking with one blue eye and one gold eye.

"Ppsst, ppsst," Bo hissed, and turned back into the saddle room. The cat leaped inside and stalked around the sacks and cans cluttering the floor.

"Ppsst—catch 'em!" Bo urged. Suddenly the cat hit—thunk—and a rush of little bones swatted the floor. Her teeth had cracked the base of the neck, gripped, and the huge rat was slung from left to right in a furious, primeval rage.

Satisfied, Bo went to the corn crib and gathered ten or twelve ears of corn and dumped them into a box for the sorrel.

He swung the back-yard gate open and treaded up the brick walk. From the gate to the house the character of the land and foliage changed. This one thing, all the shrubbery and flowers, undertaken by his wife and grumbled about by Bo himself, was in fact a secret pleasure. He had growled about having to plant and cultivate the whole thousand acres and keep up fifteen miles of fence, but he liked it all. Once in a while it was quiet enough to sit on the long back gallery, and especially then he liked it. But most of the time the damn children were screaming and yelling. He wished he had never had the first one. But you needed at least one to pass the place on to.

Now it was quiet. He did not realize his freedom at first until he got to the back door. A family man expected, was inured to, noise and commotion. Sanctuary had to be found somewhere else, away from home.

He went to the bathroom and washed the dust and grit from his hairy arms and his face, exulting in the freshness. Then he went to the icebox and took out a bottle of homebrew and poured it into a clay mug until the frothy head looked over the side.

The sun was setting as he went out again to the back gallery and propped his feet up on the railing and leaned his chair back. This batch of homebrew had come off good. A light amber, not the darkness of the last crock.

As he drank the cold beer, he thought about what he had to do the next day. More corn had to be laid by. Had to get one of the hands up with a mule in the morning to plow the garden. His wife had been after him about that. Damn woman. These two acres around this house caused him more trouble than the whole place.

He got up to get another beer and noticed that one of Mary's girls was coming down the lane. By the time she got the back gate opened he was already seated again. It was the one called Gloria. She was maybe fifteen.

"Evenin', Mista Bo." She approaching him.

"Hey, girl," looking at her.

"Mama says you want me to cook some dinner. Says Miz Simmons gone," she said, just saying anything.

"See what you can find in the icebox and go ahead and start. I'm going to take a bath."

"Yessuh." Gloria walked up the steps of the gallery and past Bo. She trailed a thick smell behind her, and it pricked the flow of Bo's thoughts. He watched her walk through the screen door and noticed the jut of her buttocks. He remembered how Louis, a field hand, had remarked about it one day when Gloria had shuffled by them on a dusty lane.

On his way to take a bath, he got another homebrew from the icebox, poured it into his mug, and started the water. He thought how much easier it was now that there was water from the cistern piped into the house. And he thought how much he enjoyed (when he was in the mood) lying in the tub and sipping a homebrew. It was not often that he felt relaxed enough. As he was washing off, he realized there was no towel.

"Damnit," he muttered. "Gloria!" He bellowed the name. A couple of rooms away she yelled back, "Suh?"

"Bring me a towel."

Soon she knocked and said, "Here it is," not opening the door.

"Well, throw it in here, girl."

She opened the door just enough to throw in the towel, but she saw in a wink Bo Simmons as few had ever seen him. There was a studied lack of recognition by both of them—a dark immobility on the girl's part, a feigned otherworldliness on his part. But the recognition was there. Bo dried off and went to his room where he found a loose-fitting shirt and a pair of khakis. He didn't bother to put a belt around him but got into some slippers.

When he came to the dining room there was a plate full of sliced cucumbers and tomatoes waiting, which he promptly set to. The scratching of his knife and fork brought Gloria to the door. After she confirmed that the boss man was there, she went back to the kitchen and came out with a big slice of fried ham on a plate and a bowl of blackeyed peas. She moved close to Bo and set them down near his salad.

"Mista Bo, did you want another homebrew, or some milk, or jest what?' she asked, looking down at him.

He thought a second and turned his face to speak and was confronted with the looming bulk of her breasts. His eyes fastened on them, and he spoke as if he was directing his request there.

"I reckon you can bring me another homebrew."

"Yessuh, hit sure do make you feel good on a hot night." But she said it with an insinuative lilt to her voice, a prerogative gainsaid now by the image in the bathroom and her cognition of Bo's last glance, a glance he had not in fact directed but rather halted.

"You can pour yourself one if you think you can handle it," not looking at her.

"Yessuh. I think I can," assuming her womanhood by the challenge, the awakened forces freed of anything servile, obedient.

The sound of caps popping on two bottles stirred Bo now to the point where there was little question whether, but only when. The problems it might bring crossed his consciousness slightly, but the alcohol quietly dismissed the future. Anyway, he was Bo Simmons.

Gloria came back to the table with a plate of french fries and a mug of homebrew. When she had placed them on the table Bo Simmons whacked her on her butt.

"Mista Bo!" she yelled, and ran out to the kitchen, leaving Bo grinning at the table.

They sure have hard rear-ends, he thought. That's what field work will do.

Before he had finished the meal, he heard the cap pop on another bottle.

"All right," he yelled, "you better go easy on the stuff!"

A quiet grunt from the kitchen. Finally she came into the dining room to clear away some of the dishes, this time from the other side of the table. Then she sat herself down in a hide-covered chair just inside the kitchen door. He ate slowly and stole glances while he chewed his food. She sat knowing he was looking, and he sat and ate, knowing that she knew.

She wet her lips with her tongue, moved it in that learned way, left her lips open. Then, as if it was part of the ritual, she began to move her crossed leg up and down gently, undulating her body in the way school girls do on the front row. Gloria had never been to school.

The flirting was easy. Perhaps for someone who had

fallen into a world of tease, this would be like any other happening. But these were not lovers, tired of the world. Her world was limited by the dirt road which she had walked coming from her cabin, the fields where she sometimes worked, the river, and now and then the house of the Simmons family. Several years ago she had been awakened to her sex by the frantic caress of a grown field hand, a friend of her father's. This had pushed back the boundaries of her world more than anything else that had ever happened to her.

And Bo. Living in a circle of work made for his own diversion, working himself away from some place inside him that was too complicated for him to understand.

The slap across the rear did not altogether make clear to Gloria where she stood. The recognition in the bathroom had been clear, and an awful excitement had engulfed her; that was substantial. But men had taken the license Bo Simmons had taken before and meant nothing, except to make clear what was theirs or could be if they wanted it.

It was time. Bo finished his supper and she picked up the few remaining dishes and went to the sink. Bo followed her and as he came up behind her, held onto her hips.

"Mista Bo, you gotta stop now," looking straight ahead, not confident, a little afraid.

"Never mind bout all that, girl. Forget them dishes and get on in here with me." He started out of the kitchen.

She didn't move, only moistened her lips that kept drying. He turned, looked at her strangely, then grabbed her wrist and pulled her along with him. She did not pull back, neither did she move forward on her own, but kept her feet dragging under her, so he would know it was all his doing.

"Take your clothes off, girl," he said and sat down heavily on the side of the mammoth tester bed. There were solid oak posts ten inches at the base and a brownness that spoke of permanence and stability. The bed had come from a prominent home when the family failed. His back to her, he undressed, threw his clothes on the nearby stand, and finally stood there naked. He started out of the room, said, "You better have that dress off before I get back or I'll tan your hide. I'm gonna git us some more homebrew."

When he came back, her plain dress was on the floor and she was sitting in the rocking chair next to the fireplace, the ashes gunbarrel gray, cold, the fires long out. She had settled there out of habit, as if being there was a comfort to her. He handed her a clay mug, and she got up and followed him to the bed.

After he had possessed her and she had exhausted him, he napped with his head resting on her big breasts. His knees were pulled up close to him in a position unseemly for a man so big. She did not sleep but remained staring at the designs of stars and new moons in the canopy above her. The face was young and her cheeks had the fullness of a young woman, but something about her reflected a knowledge that had been beaten to shape and tempered long before this small fire had been lit. In the midst of her dark, shadowy lap lay his calloused hand, the digits slightly curved to the grip of an ax, or a gun.

For a while the young woman did not think of much beyond the bed. With her head propped on the pillow she could study his head, the long, brown hair with silver sides like the silver-sided fox she had heard his dog hunt, his neck reddened by years in the sun. She stared almost uncomprehendingly at the sudden change to the child-like alabaster skin covering his torso, an awful whiteness, sharp against her own dark body.

But the heat and their half-dried, perspiring bodies soon forced her to other thoughts. How she had cleaned and swept this room and made this bed for Mrs. Simmons, never seeing the room like this. For some reason the thought of chores reminded her of her mother and she reflexively moved one of her legs. Bo stirred and pulled his whiskered face across her chest, straightened out his legs, and lay on his back. His eyes were open, but he didn't say anything for a while.

When he ran his hands along the lines of her body, she didn't move. Something in his touch reassured her. She waited, knew now that he was awake, that the next move had to be his. She did not think what it would be and did not want to care.

"You better git on home now," he said, and his words were heavy in the thick air of the room. She rolled out of bed, the shape of her naked body barely visible against the papered wall. She got dressed in the dark.

She didn't look at him again and went out of the room quickly, not bothering to close the door. On the back steps she could hear the Brahmas lowing across the fields. The man's voice reached out to her where she stood.

"Don't you tell anybody bout this."

"Nosuh Mista Bo," she said. "I ain gone tell nobody." And she moved from the darkness of the house to the darkness of the road, where she knew her way.

A Marquis

Tuck LaFleur was a short man and he had the problems of short men. We called him a "banty rooster," though not to his face. During a good bit of school he was forever putting on the gloves with somebody.

His daddy and mother worked for the state insane asylum in those days, and that had a lot to do with his raising. His daddy, a short fellow too, had the reputation of running a tough ward. He'd as soon lay a patient out as look at him, or so the talk went. Tuck's parents working for the state separated him from a lot of other boys. Their daddys were independent farmers. As far as the farmers were concerned, anyone who lived on their tax money was a parasite.

LaFleur disappeared after graduation and most of us lost track of him. It was known by those who cared about knowing that he worked for the "Federal Government," and somehow it was circulated that he was a spy or something. The men down at the service station said they didn't know of anyone better suited than a Frenchman, and besides LaFleur was little and hard to catch.

One holiday season he came back for two weeks and stayed at his mama's long enough to sweep Constance Wintertree off her feet.

Constance was from one of the first or second families in town and everyone had expected her to marry a doctor from the asylum. A young woman built like Constance surely would not be wasted on a rough farmer's son. She was a foot taller than LaFleur, and the one time we saw them together, the old heads shook sadly. No one could figure the attraction.

Then they left, married. For ten years there were only occasional letters from Constance and never anything about what Tuck was doing. Constance's mama said they changed addresses often. The Wintertrees didn't say much but everyone could tell they felt they had thrown pearls to swine.

Suddenly the LaFleurs returned. And it wasn't long before we knew Tuck was going to build a barroom.

All of the parish was not dry. Any ward could vote liquor in if it wanted to, but the women ignored the one or two little wet places. LaFleur bought a patch of woods right next to the ward line of Bethel and proved to the people that a Frenchman would do anything for money.

There was talk that maybe something would happen like had happened to Ben Jacob's honky-tonk, which was burned to the ground early one Sunday morning so everybody could get an idea on the way to church of what happens to somebody who sells booze in the second ward.

But LaFleur built his bar, not caring about or not hearing the soft, furious words. Maybe he had been vaccinated against small towns by wherever he had been. Further, he built it mostly with his own hands. We knew he didn't know anything about building. He would ask some jakeleg carpenter a question about pitching a roof and off he'd go. Then he'd stare at a brickmason for a day or two and take a stab at bricklaying (which had to be straightened out later on).

He had picked up a lot of other ideas from somewhere else because gradually as the building rose we knew it wasn't going to be like Connell's shack by the sawmill. At Connell's there was one long wooden bench and a woodstove. LaFleur had a big stone chimney running up the side of the building. It wasn't long before a machine was building a lake out in back. Then we weren't sure what he was building. Some said probably Sheriff Thompson wouldn't issue the license and come the first of the year LaFleur would have that fine building and nothing to do. Besides, Protestant ladies said nobody would go but Mandeville trash anyhow.

But this was all by the way. Before New Year's everyone knew the license had been granted. And one thing we had forgotten: Constance Wintertree's legions of relatives. That is, not only Wintertrees but Fitzsimmons, Farleys, and Tomes—just in the immediate family. All were known to take a drink. Then there was Tuck's kin that he did not know, since he was in the hills and they were down in the bayou country. Well when folks saw that so many people were bound to come and that one of the deputy sheriffs, Carl Rodney, was going to be there because he was Constance's cousin on her mother's side, a whole pack of us came. Others went as people do when the last few whooping cranes come to Louisiana—just to be there so they could talk about it when it was gone.

We all went dressed up because by now we understood that this was to be no juke-joint. That wives would even be there. After we walked in we were glad we had come dressed. In the crowd that was already gathered you could see dresses that were worn once maybe to the American Legion dance over at Choctaw or to high school graduation. Red necks bulged over white collars and nearly all of the men were dressed better than they usually did, except for weddings and funerals. But the inside of the bar was a wonder. We all knew of such bars, but most of us had never been in one. Tuck had big cypress rafters and pine paneling on the walls. And the fireplace looked like it was big enough to heat the high school gym. There were four man-size logs on the fire, and it looked like it could hold more than that. Around the fireplace a lot of the couples were sitting at wooden tables. Most of the bachelors and young men were drinking at the long, polished bar.

The bar wasn't new. It was made like the big sideboards and armoires of an earlier time, with hand-carved flowers and faces leering from the top. Great mirrors were inlaid in the sideboard and surrounded by gilded frames.

Connell's stocked beer, two or three bourbons, and one brand of gin, but all over Tuck's shelves were bottles many of us hadn't even heard of: Irish whiskey, cognac, wines, liqueurs—every color of alcohol. A lot of the women were drinking these drinks, the colored ones. Up and down the bar and on the tables were cheese, crackers, pickles, and little squares of meat on toothpicks. The cheese was on thick cutting boards, each with its own knife. All of the food was free.

At one end of the room and between the tables and the bar was a place to dance, and the couples glowed eerily in the colored lights as they passed the new Wurlitzer nickelodeon. Some of the songs were of an older day, but we discovered later that Tuck wouldn't change them even if customers wouldn't play them, or if they asked him to change them. This was only a hint of his mule-headedness.

Constance had put on a little weight, but she was as beautiful as ever. She even looked foreign. She wore a dress in an oriental style that went nearly to the floor, white with silvery beads sewn to the material. She fairly shimmered. The high collar set off her dark, tanned face.

Naturally all of us were looking at her. LaFleur was looking at everything else that wiggled, but wasn't leering. He just looked as if he was checking stock, more because men expect another man to look full square at a big-breasted, hip-flaring female to show he is all right than because he is aching inside.

The wee hours came on, and the family types left. The hardcore drinkers who would sustain LaFleur in the coming days remained, and he seemed to loosen up. In fact he got a little drunk. As if he had reached a place he had been trying to get to. When there were only a dozen left, he asked Constance to dance. She came from behind the bar, and they began to dance alone. Everyone seemed to wait, allowing royalty to call the pace. Then, two or three couples moved onto the floor, swaying to the quiet music in the smoky bar.

When the song ended, the couples stopped on the floor and LaFleur and Constance began talking to them. The music started, and Buck Morgan's wife, Sarah, stacked like a brick shithouse, said, "Tuck, honey, dance with me."

He grinned and said, "All right Sarah Lee, it'd be my pleasure." This left Sarah's husband, Buck Morgan, nothing to do but take Constance's hand and begin to dance. She fell to her task so that Buck was all taken up for the rest of the dance.

Tuck clearly enjoyed himself what with Sarah Lee tight on him as bark on an elm tree, especially when Buck had his back to them. This started a round of dancing. At first all the couples exchanged partners, but then Sarah Lee asked Buck's brother Jessie to dance and soon the other single fellows started in. It was about this time that we noticed Tuck glancing at Constance. She was having the time of her life, not being out of the way, but bubbling over.

Tuck quit dancing. He went behind the bar to fix another round for everybody and he stayed. Constance would return once in a while to fill up her glass and Tuck didn't have anything to say. He picked up his drinking though, and his eyes got glassy. It was as if some kind of switch had clicked. His face sagged as if somebody had hit him with a maul.

When Constance returned the next time, she noticed him and she seemed to change. She didn't leave the bar either. The talk kept up at a fast, raucous clip, but something had been pulled out of the air and soon everyone, staggering numb-happy, was screeching their best wishes and good fortune to this worthy enterprise, under the blinking stars. As we left there was little Tuck standing with his hands in his pockets and Constance in her tight, oriental dress, lofty against her husband, the mist rising on the lake behind them in backdrop.

The days went by as they always had, but for many of us the procession now seemed to move around Tuck's place. It was almost like church and we had our own preacher. Every weekend there would be a cookout of some kind by the lake bank. Couples, young and old, ate at long cypress-planked tables under the strings of light that led to the water's edge. Crawfish season came in the spring and Tuck would go deep in the French country and bring back a pickup truck load of the crawling red shellfish. They had to have pieces of ice around them to keep them from dying, and when he got them back to the place he built a fire under a hugh black pot and dumped them into the boiling water. The smell of the seasoning, the red peppers and onions and lemons, drifted over the lawn, and we wondered if spring had ever been this fine. Our hands, sticky from peeling the mounds of crawfish on the tables before us, smeared handles of the mugs of beer, but we didn't care.

The girls, after a drink or two, sang several-part harmony,

thinking they sounded grand, even singing church hymns, because these songs were the only ones they knew by heart—harmony, because the church had taught them that, too.

The youngest men and women were caught up in the eating and drinking, the new green of the trees, and before the evening was very old, it having started perhaps at three in the afternoon, they finally would stagger drunk to their cars and roar off into the night, either to wrap themselves around a pine tree or in each other's arms if chance led them to a deserted lane they had known since childhood.

The older folks, the married couples and the strange, eccentric bachelors, the hard core, enjoyed themselves, too, but with a restraint that kept them going and maybe a foreknowledge that this good time, this new place would have an end to it like so many others had. These were the ones that watched Tuck and Constance the closest and were the first to detect a strangeness between them.

Maybe the free time to drink every day and night started to tell on them, but Tuck and Constance felt they had to get away from the bar occasionally. Down the highway towards Baton Rouge was a golf course right out in the middle of nowhere, its site chosen by a land-speculating golf pro, and one or the other of them would play golf during the week. Both couldn't leave the bar. Besides, they had tried playing together on Sundays with some of the couples that drank at the bar, but the outings were not always enjoyable. Golfers are funny people, and these didn't enjoy Tuck's repeated criticism of Constance. Not that she was inept. As a matter of fact she played, according to these people, as well as Tuck. Both were very good. While Tuck was busy doing whatever he did for the government, Constance had played golf in every town around the world where she had to stay, even winning the ladies' division in a few amateur tournaments. But when she missed any kind of shot, Tuck would make some comment. If she made a better score, his explanation was to the effect that while he had had to work for ten years, she lolled in country clubs. But she never said a word.

As she and Tuck tried to play more golf, Constance didn't feel like cleaning up the bar after the nightly storm, and then polishing all the bottles once a week. (The menfolk said among themselves that she would never polish bottles if they had their way, haw haw.) She complained in front of the whole bar one night and Tuck was pushed into Lewis Durham's suggestion that they use Ida Mae, their maid. That she was a very good worker. Tightly quiet and grudgingly, Tuck said all right. But he wouldn't look at Constance. Tuck only began drinking harder.

The older folks started drifting away first. Imperceptibly. Someone would ask where was old man Turner, that they hadn't seen him lately, and a volunteer would offer the excuse: he was getting in hay, or he was pulling corn—they thought. Gradually customers were watching other customers. Some wife would look at her husband quickly as Tuck made smart remarks to Constance. She was getting fat, he said. She was drinking all day and night. When was she going to get off her lard ass. For these couples, the unfolding marital battlefield, before them on the narrow runway behind the bar, excited some fearful parts of themselves— and they left quietly and often for good.

The young, having no real knowlege of these things, stayed on. Tuck's tongue lashings of this beautiful woman were their excitement. The young, knotty-muscled men looked like fresh dogs excited by the bloody spoor of a fat young doe. Things came loose in them they would call by many names, never what they were.

And the young, tough, red-clay hussies rolled their eyes, thinking, this will never be me and my man, but maybe even they were hypnotized for moments by this old, old story. Changing like weathervanes, however, these dungareed wenches could dance before one nickelodeon as well as another. Soon Tuck's only business was their spasmodic raids—that and his sidedoor colored business. But then they could be what-do-you-want-boyed at any number of places.

Long after the novelty had worn off and hours of pot-bellied gossip had fitted this piece in the parish mosaic, a certain story curled like wispy blue smoke over and through the trees, down dusty lanes, and furtively through the gravel streets of Bethel. It was hard to know for sure, but it didn't somehow matter—the story ought to have been true anyway. Whatever had happened, the knowledge of it had ripened, fermented in the quarter, but needed a lot of time to force its way across that ungray line between black folks and white. Maybe it was the intersectional clearinghouse, the gray-sheeted bed of one of the Crawford brothers that had served up this delicacy. For between one or another of the Crawfords and legions of maids, a part of the charm of the old South still lived.

Ida Mae told only her mother. Maybe scared, maybe sometimes grinning unbelieving. Thursday morning she went to work as usual. Mr. Tuck's truck was gone when she got there, but there was a note on the door to her: "Ida Mae, go ahead in and go to work." She went on in and started to work, not because of the note, she couldn't read, but before when she had seen her name on another note, she had remained outside on the steps and Mr. Tuck had gotten terrible angry and cussed when he came back. Then she knew the note had said to go in and clean up. This morning was cold and gray, but there was a small fire already started in the big fireplace. She added a little wood and soon the blaze was flickering shapes to the empty and always dimly lighted barroom. She poured all the ashtrays on the cluttered floor, wiped the shining bar clean, and then swept the whole floor. Next she washed all of the glasses, there weren't many, and finally started on the many, many colored bottles along the shelves back of the bar. The cloth she used to dust with was too dirty, though, and she started to the back of the place to get another from the linen pantry when she heard what sounded like a bottle fall to the floor and a stirring from Mr. Tuck's bedroom. She didn't know what to do. Her tongue became dry and scratchy and her heart pounded and pounded. Oh Jesus, oh Jesus!

"Who's that?" hiding behind the loudness of her question.

She peeped around the corner of the little hall and saw a cat moving to the door and pushing it open enough to slip past. Maybe it was a rat.

She padded softly to the bedroom door and looked through the crack. In the dim bluish light of the room was Miz Constance, naked and leaning over the side of the bed reaching for a small bottle. She saw Ida Mae through the crack.

"Oh, Miz Constance, I didn't know it was you," she said, not now looking in the crack.

"Are you about finished?" came the question in a husky-throated voice.

"Yessum, just a little bit more."

"You might as well come in here a minute," she ordered, a little weakly.

Ida Mae pushed the door open and before her Miz Constance's broad-hipped white body seemed to fill the bed, the first white female body she had ever seen. She was lying on her back holding the little bottle in a limp hand over her soft breasts.

"Rub this oil on me," and handed her the bottle.

Ida unscrewed the pretty, half-used bottle and could smell a beautiful scent.

Slowly the woman in bed turned her hips, then her whole body, so she lay on her stomach. And in the dim half-light, red and blue narrow welts screamed out to the Negro girl. All over the shapely back the thin criss-cross lines stared, becoming more abundant across her buttocks.

82

"Ohhh me," moaned Ida Mae, "Missy, Missy."

"Never mind. Just rub the oil on me," said the sleep-creased, dusky face, her luxuriant dark hair spilling along the pillow.

The black hands began to move up and down, up and down, stopping to fill with the sweet-scented oil, then covering all the flesh except where she was too timid to touch.

"When you finish, go on home, Ida," said the woman already sleepy.

"Yessum."

And as she screwed the top on the delicate bottle and put it on the night stand, her mistress's mouth was beginning to pout in unconscious sleep, with a faint smile at the corner of her lips.

To Pass Him Out

◆⊰ ⊱◆

"Come in, come in Mabel. And who's that you have with you?" she asked in a violent whisper. A ten-year-old boy followed Mabel Bauman in off the front gallery and through the hall.

"This is Tommy, my sister Julie's child. Tommy's visiting with us this summer. Wanted to see what country life was like. Say hello, Tommy," demanded Mabel Bauman, following her friend into the front parlor.

"Hello, ma'am," chimed Tommy automatically. The house had funny smells. Everything was old.

"Miz Fanny," said Aunt Mabel, then hesitating to give weight, "How is Mr. Tillman? We've been so worried."

Aunt Mabel didn't know Mr. Tillman very well, but Uncle Jack had said Mr. Tillman owned a big farm out of Bethel. That he took sick way back in the woods on his place and there was nobody to take care of him but a pack of niggers living on the place. Mrs. Fanny told some of the ladies in the church to bring Mr. Tillman to her house (even if he didn't want to come) and she'd take care of him.

"Just hanging on, Mabel, just hanging on. He had a troublesome night. I just don't know how he does it. The poor dear is so weak, but he's got a will, you know. You can just see it in his eyes. I remember my second husband, Mr. Steele, before he went to his reward. His eyes seemed so quiet—" she paused, her eyes looking off to see the scene, "quiet with acceptance—but now Emmett Tillman is a different man."

Then she suddenly turned her attention to the boy. "How would you like a glass of cold buttermilk, young man?"

"Now, Miz Fanny, he doesn't need a thing. Don't you bother yourself. I just wanted to visit a minute and maybe sneak a few lilies for the church. That's such a fine bed you have out front."

"Help yourself to anything you see, Mabel. But it's no bother at all to get this young man a glass of buttermilk. I'll get you some shears, and you can be doing that while I go to the kitchen."

No one had bothered getting the boy's answer, did he want some buttermilk.

Mrs. Fanny trudged down the hall to the back of the house. The boy's aunt took the shears and went out to cut flowers, leaving him suddenly alone with Mrs. Fanny. She hummed a fragment of a hymn as she opened the icebox. Taking a gallon crock from inside, she poured the frothy buttermilk into a big glass. He watched the yellow flecks of butter swirl around as she placed the glass in front of him and said, "There." As she did so she leaned close to him and the inside of her dressing gown folded open just enough so part of her breast showed. It was whiter than the brown, freckled skin of her throat and there were little blue veins near the nipple, but he could not see the nipple.

He swallowed his saliva as she drew away, no sign that she knew he had seen, no sign that she even cared whether he had seen. She said, "That ought to hold you. There's more if you want it."

He said, "Yessum." He started to drink, tasting it gingerly. He had never drunk buttermilk before and was not prepared for the acrid taste. He wrinkled his nose.

"It's a little sour. Is that the way it's supposed to taste?" he asked.

"Let me see," and picked up his glass, taking a taste. "Why sure. That's good and fresh."

He took the glass and held it, she still looking, but he was thinking about where her old lips had touched the glass, marked harshly by the drying buttermilk.

"It'll do you good, besides being good," she said, he not believing.

"Well, now, it's time for Mr. Tillman's medicine," she announced. "You just go right ahead and drink your buttermilk," she insisted. She opened a wooden cabinet over the sink and took down two bottles of pills. Then she poured out one red and two yellow ones. She took a glass from another cupboard and placed all of this on a silver tray.

He had decided while she was doing this that the only way was to drink this buttermilk like he would milk of magnesia. Block out as much taste, smell, sight as possible, scrunch up the inside of your head until your ears rang like the wind was blowing. Then gulp, trying to will no feeling in your mouth. And he did.

Mrs. Fanny turned around carrying the tray just as he set the glass on the table.

"My, my. You must of been thirsty," she said, putting the tray down again saying, "Let me get you some more."

"No ma'am. I'm filled up." Oh don't make me drink any more, please, please.

"All right," said Mrs. Fanny.

She shuffled out of the kitchen and down the hall to Mr. Tillman's room. He got up from the table and took his glass to the sink and rinsed it out. Just like his mother. Have to drink this. Have to eat kidney stew. Ugh.

He saw an ancient picture in the big hall through the kitchen door and walked over to it. It was an old man in a high white collar and gold-rimmed glasses.

The hall floor was unpainted in the middle from years and years of walking to the bathroom at the end of the hall and the kitchen. The great hall had a high ceiling. The wallpaper was no longer snug against the wall but hung like the loose flesh on a fat woman's arms. The brown, liver-looking water spots all over the ceiling and walls were now like permanent decorations. They seemed to belong with the brown-yellowness and thick musty air of the house, smelling almost like a funeral home he had visited once. These were special smells like some other houses he'd visited in this town.

The pine boards creaked as Mrs. Fanny came from the bedroom. She was humming a Methodist hymn as she carried a white enamel bedpan in front of her. Long used to the odor of urine and human feces, she did not wrinkle her nose. The smell lingered on her waddling train of air. Cleaning noises came from the bathroom and then she came out.

"I'll be through in just a minute, son. Soon as I fix up Mr. Tillman," she said, noticing him looking at the picture.

"Who is this?" he asked.

"That's a picture of Dr. Couvillion, my husband," she replied, as she re-entered the room.

He puzzled about that. Couvillion? Why was her name Steele?

When she came out she said, "I was his nurse in the hospital in New Orleans and we got married there." She paused half-pensively, "That was many years ago. There's just me doing the nursing now."

He was faintly embarrassed by some of this conversation, but he said, "Yessum." What happened to her husbands?

"Why don't you say hello to Mr. Tillman? He doesn't get to see many people now cause he sleeps so much and he'd enjoy it. He won't be able to say much, though," and she ushered him into the room.

The shades were drawn, but there was still enough light to see. There in a bed lay the old man, his head propped up high enough that the immense oak headboard seemed to frame his gray-covered skull. His eyes flickered with interest as the boy followed Mrs. Fanny into the room.

"Tommy, this is Mr. Tillman. Emmett, this is Mabel's nephew. He's visiting us in Bethel this summer," said Mrs. Fanny.

The old man croaked out, "Hello . . . boy," and moved his hand as if to shake hands. The boy reached and took it in his own and shook it once. The knuckles were big and the hand was bent in the peculiar way of arthritis.

"How do you do, sir," answered Tommy. He didn't know what to say.

The old man tried to urge something else out, but the boy couldn't understand.

"Sir?" embarrassed.

"What's that, Emmett?" demanded Mrs. Fanny, louder than Tommy thought necessary.

Mr. Tillman's chest began to heave convulsively. "Huuh . . . huuh." His yellow eyes began rolling wildly, and he coughed, racking his thin body, barely visible underneath

89

the crocheted coverlet. Some of the phlegm in his eyes caught in his eyelashes. Mrs. Fanny reached over with her fingers and wiped them and then wiped the phlegm on her dressing gown.

The coughing subsided a moment and she said, "Come on, son, let's let Mr. Tillman rest." Mr. Tillman looked at him forlornly, Tommy thought, as if the old man didn't want him to leave, as if he had something to tell him.

Mrs. Fanny was fingering the coverlet. "I crocheted this a long time ago. Do you like it?" she asked Tommy, apparently no longer interested in the man.

"Yessum."

"Come see the one on my bed," and led the way into the hall and into the adjoining room. There was a door between the two, but on Mrs. Fanny's side there was an old armoire blocking the way.

"This one took me long hours to do, but I've always liked it," she said, moving her palm over the coverlet caressingly.

On one wall near the foot of her tester bed was a picture that the boy looked at briefly. It hung so that it could be seen if someone was lying in the bed. There were two figures, a young man and a young woman. They were in postures of affectionate adoration. The young woman had a misty face, hard ivory cheeks with a rouged blush of innocence, and long blond hair hung to her bosom at which point the man's head, covered with blond ringlets, lay in divine repose.

Above the head of the bed a picture of Jesus hung so that no one could see it lying down in bed. It was on a calendar and was one of those views of Jesus with a bright red valentine heart that glistened on his outer garments. The year of the calendar caught the boy's attention because it was before he was even born.

Mrs. Fanny had big hands and wrists. They looked out of

place as she picked up some little porcelain figurines and showed them to him.

"These are some from my house in New Orleans."

He turned them over in his hands and nodded. He wished he was back over at the service station talking to his friend Gene. His daddy ran the service station and Gene worked there on Saturdays. The big cow trucks and farm tractors pulled in for gas and oil. Gene's daddy said it was all right for him to help put the gas in and wipe the windshields. A lot of the men parked their pickups near the station and came in just to talk. There were several coke cases to sit on and one chair near the coke machine. Some of the men shot long streams of tobacco juice near the stove that wasn't working. Tommy wished he were there watching them. He felt uneasy.

The back door slammed, and he could hear his Aunt Mabel in the kitchen. Mrs. Fanny looked very slightly annoyed but said, "Let's go see what your aunt has got." She put her arm around his shoulders and walked by him to the kitchen. He thought he would die, but then he remembered her breast and even though he was uncomfortable, he felt pleasingly warm. He insisted to himself, however, that he wanted to get away. She dropped her arm before they came to Aunt Mabel.

"Oh, Miz Fanny, everything was so fresh and beautiful, I just hated to cut anything. But just look at them. Aren't they nice?" She had an arm load of white lilies spread out on newspaper on the kitchen table. The yellow pollen was dusted over the big round insides and made Tommy almost heady as Mrs. Fanny offered one for him to smell. He took the one she offered him and juicy sap stained his hand. It was sticky and a little perplexing. He wanted to wipe his hands on his pants, but he couldn't, so it dried there. Most of the other thick stems were together and looked like asparagus in a glass jar.

"Let me help you put them in water, Mabel," and the two women busied themselves with their chore.

Again he thought of the service station. While he was there this morning, before Aunt Mabel came and got him, he had told Gene he had to go with his aunt to Mrs. Fanny's. Some of the men sitting around the station had heard him and started talking about her among themselves. He had overheard them discussing all the land she had inherited and then they laughed. One of the men spoke up and said, "Don't you all let me end up with her nursing me if I get down." They laughed again. Why were they laughing? They mentioned Mr. Tillman, too, that before long Miz Fanny would *pass him out*. He didn't know what that meant.

"Well, now, they'll look real nice for Easter services, won't they, Miz Fanny," commented Aunt Mabel. "You're going to be able to come, aren't you?"

"It doesn't look like it, Mabel, honey. Mercy me, I'll have to be here with Emmett. And I know everyone is going to be there, too. But I just don't see how. But my lilies will be there anyway."

"Well, don't you fret. I'll mention you to everybody," she said and then turned to Tommy. "So, youngun, let's us go. Take some of the flowers." He did as he was told.

"Thank Miz Fanny for the buttermilk."

"Thank you for the buttermilk and everything," he murmured.

"You come back and see me, you hear," and she pressed his thin shoulder with her arm.

He and his aunt walked along the gravel street to their house. He waved across the railroad track to Gene at the service station and hoped he didn't look too sissified carrying a vase of flowers and walking by his aunt.

Promise

+9 6+

Jason sped north on the blacktop in his topless jeep through the late Louisiana morning. He was vaguely hung over and was falling behind. Jimmy Davis had rattled up in the yard earlier and yelled from the truck, "Mr. Bo said you could come up to the north catchpen," and then roared off. Jason had gone back to sleep. He wouldn't be late now if he hadn't run into Lou Beth at the bar last night. Just when he was going to leave she came in, walked over, gave him a hug, and said she felt like dancing. Lou Beth was an old friend, and besides she was an armful of woman. How could he refuse?

The night had a twist in it though and so did Lou Beth.

It became clear she wasn't hanging tight to him out of off-hand healthy exuberance; her life had hit a dead end. She didn't come out with it, but while she was getting cigarettes from the machine, the bar owner, LaFleur, who knew everybody's business, remarked that she got the shaft from a married man she had been seeing. Jason didn't say anything about it to her, just kept on dancing, keeping his arms around her big healthy body. Her breasts seemed fuller, her middle stouter. Playfully, he told her she was putting on a little weight.

"Thanks a lot, Jason," and she stalked out of the bar. He thought she would just smart-mouth him right back and was surprised when she got mad. The female was very mysterious, he thought.

As he pulled the jeep up in a small cloud of dust by the catchpen, the humidity, the hangover, the hot sun all seemed to beat him down. Tied to one of the catchpen's posts was a two-year-old heifer. Her rear end was toward him, but she turned her head around to see what was happening, and her Brahma eyes rolled wildly in their sockets. Her back was arched, her legs spread like she was going to let loose.

Standing next to her was a tall, powerfully built man. His striped shirt was unbuttoned part way down, showing a wide field of black hair, mottled with gray. A stranger would judge him to be fifty. Jason stayed in the jeep, not saying anything, just looking at the older man who was not looking at him. Neither spoke. Jason watched him scrape his boots across the lowest board of the catchpen.

Finally: "Well, stud, how is everything?" said Jason, violating the quiet sultriness of the summer day—a moment when there was nothing mechanical going on, no man sound on the edge of the woods.

"I see you finally dragged your ass out of bed," the man said.

Jason grinned a little, still not getting out of the jeep. "Looks like you beat me up."

"Huh! That wouldn't take much."

"I got hung up at LaFleur's last night," Jason explained.

"Yeah," he said knowingly. "Looks like we left one of those heifers in this herd. They always give you trouble. I'd rather fool with an old mama cow than a young heifer ain't never had a calf. This one's tryin to—and tryin is about the end of it. I suspect we'll lose both of em fore the day's over. Ain't hardly worth foolin with." His voice was fatalistic and flat.

"Just don't let my half die."

"You layin your lard ass up in the bed and then worrying about *your* half. If it was up to me I'd shoot her and give her to the dogs."

And he could, too, Jason thought, but he won't. "What we gonna do?"

"I told Jimmy Davis to go get my medicine box and a cable." Jimmy Davis was a black parolee on work release. He was just eighteen and had promised Bo he would work hard if he took him. Bo knew where to get cheap help. He had been in the pen himself.

"What'd you need the cable for?"

"Have to pull it out with the jeep maybe."

"How in the world you gonna do that?"

"You'll see soon enough."

The heifer lowed unhappily in her separation from the herd, and from deep in the woods came the low, guttural answer of an older, full-blooded Brahma cow. Jason knew Bo liked that sound, the sound of an ancient and powerful line. Jason had not been able to identify it a year ago, when he was just starting in the cow business. He had asked "What was that?" straight off, and Bo laughed unkindly and said it was a dragon. Then an old mama cow lumbered into view, looking for her calf.

95

"All right, doll, help's on the way. Soon as that skinny-ass Jimmy Davis gets here." Bo talked to the heifer, and she looked like she understood him. Jason liked that about fooling with cows, the closeness you felt with the animals. Somehow you could get closer to animals without all the complications you had with people.

"You can be turning the jeep around so we can tie on soon as he gets here." Jason started doing what he was told, not really understanding yet what was to take place. He had learned to do what he was told, wanted to do what he was told, because he knew he was still an apprentice. He was a partner only because Bo took a liking to him. He didn't have much to contribute except his labor and a nonchalance about signing mortgages that would have scared older men to death, men with wives and children.

And then he did what Bo told him to because Bo was a professional. He would have been a veterinarian, but you had to go to school to do that, and Bo just made it to the tenth grade when he kicked his books all the way home, which was about a mile, and didn't go back. It wasn't long after that he went to the pen. A buddy of his who promised to drive the getaway car got scared and left him holding the bag. It was in the pen he learned most of the cow-doctoring he knew. When he got paroled and went into the business, he doctored his own animals.

For most things he was as good as the vet. People called on him because he didn't charge anything . . . not at first, anyway. They just became obligated. In these days a lot of people kept cattle for fun or taxes, and didn't know how to treat their own animals. Jason respected Bo because he knew a pro when he saw one and he knew a vet bill would break him.

It would take a while for Jimmy Davis to get back because this was the northernmost pasture—most of their land was leased and strung out over twenty miles. After Jason finished turning the jeep around he got out and sat down on the ground. Bo came over by him, eased himself down, and propped up against the back tire.

"Her water bag's already broke."

"How long can we wait?" Jason asked. He knew that after the water broke, the calf had to come out in an hour or two.

"I don't know exactly. It shoulda already been out. You can bet it's hung up." Bo shook his head dramatically. "So you laid out with the dry cattle last night, huh?"

"I was just gonna have one beer, you know. Then Lou Beth came in all fouled up. She was in the dumps and throwing bourbon down like tomorrow was prohibition. I don't know what her trouble is. LaFleur said some married man she's been seeing gave her the shaft. You heard anything about that?"

"Oh, seems like that was in the grapevine. Course, I try to stay away from all that. Leave it to you young people."

"She got all mad at me just cause I joked she was putting on weight. Of course, she has a little."

"You got real tact. Maybe she had help putting on that weight."

"You don't think . . . ?"

The rattle of the pickup interrupted them as Jimmy Davis bumped into view. "Where you been, son?" Bo asked, not expecting a real answer, Jimmy Davis knowing he wasn't expected to give one.

"Had to find the medicine box, Mr. Bo."

"Bring it over here. What you waiting on?" Jimmy Davis put the box down where Bo stood. Bo took out a thin stainless steel cable and put it on the back of the jeep. Then he drew out two long transparent plastic gloves. He pulled off his shirt and hung it over the top catchpen board. Although he had a big chest, there was still a roll of fat above his belt line, and Jason could tell he was a little self-conscious about it, as most men were. He unrolled the gloves and pulled them up to his armpits.

He crouched behind the heifer, the hurt having dulled her caring, and reached inside her, his right arm so far in he had to turn his face to the side. He groped around, trying to feel shape, bone, tissue.

"Well, at least the damn thing is pointed in the right direction. But her bones are just not wide enough, or her baby's too big. That's why I never like to screw around with a heifer."

"Is that why the head is so big?" chortled Jason. Jimmy Davis didn't understand but laughed because Jason had.

"Never mind. Jimmy Davis, gimme that cable and git to stirrin around," Bo said, ignoring Jason, moving to the task like a doctor in surgery. He took the cable and formed a noose, his right arm slimy now with the clinging plastic glove. Then into the heifer with the cable.

"Watcha gonna do now?" Jason asked.

"Got to fasten this around the legs," never taking his eyes from the heifer. "And then we got to pull." Occasionally his left hand entered the opening to help, then back out. A couple of times Jason almost laughed at Bo's face jammed against the heifer's rear end, but thought better of it.

"OK. Now we work."

"You want me to back the jeep up closer?" Jason asked.

"No. We ain't gonna use it now. I hope we don't have to. If she tries some more, we'll just pull when she labors. But I don't know. This girl looks like she ain't got much push left in her."

The afternoon sun thickened the air to a gumbo as Bo and Jason sat on the bumper of the jeep to wait. Jason thought about last night and Lou Beth. Funny she never mentioned anything about seeing anybody steady. Why get mixed up with a married man? She was just eighteen. That couldn't lead anywhere. Just a dead end. What if what Bo said was true? He always seemed to know to look beneath the surface of things.

Just then the heifer strained. Jason held the cable taut and Bo held the heifer. They leaned back in a crazy tug-of-war. As Jason pulled, the cable seemed to give some and he hollered.

"I think it's coming!"

"Let go!" Bo yelled. "Let go, quick!"

"What's the matter?" Bo didn't answer. He started putting on his glove again. "What's the matter?" Jason demanded, exasperated now.

"The noose slipped down to the hooves. They're too soft to take the cable. Crack 'em right off."

"Let me feel up in there," Jason said.

"Just a minute."

"I don't have to use that glove on my arm, do I?" not liking what he thought of as artificial things, plastic or rubber.

"Unless you want to catch something surenuff. You have any broken places on your hand or arm, you can catch things you never heard of."

Jason put on a fresh glove from the medicine box and slipped his hand into the heifer's body. He knew where to move because he could follow the cable with his fingers. Although this was new, he felt comfortable searching around inside. Suddenly he ran into the forefeet.

"I can feel the feet," he said, excited.

"Move on up the legs and you can see where the noose is."

"Yeah, I feel it."

"We better quit screwin with her now. She's about fagged out."

Bo made a motion like he was going to smear his slimy gloved hand in Jason's face. Jason leaped around the side of the jeep. "Go on, lightnin!" Bo was laughing now.

"OK, bastard!" Jason bellowed. He managed to laugh, too.

They peeled off their gloves. Jimmy Davis, who had been resting in the shadow of the jeep, got to his feet when Jason nearly trampled him.

"Jimmy Davis, take the jeep to Miss Ella's and get us some cheese and crackers and a few bottles of Miller's," Bo ordered, wiping the sweat from his head.

"Can I have one, too, Mr. Bo?"

"You can get a coke," not looking at him.

"Yessuh," half-dejectedly, but expecting the answer. It was a condition of his parole.

When Jimmy Davis returned a little while later, Bo took two of the clear bottles out of the paper bag, rolled the top of the bag tight, and put it in the shade. Then he took one of the numerous openers from the glove compartment and opened the glistening bottles, yellow in the sun, and passed one to Jason. The day had worn on, and Jason was dry and hungry. He gulped the first swallow or two, draining half the bottle.

"Glory," he sighed happily.

Bo took out his pocketknife and wiped the big blade on the pant leg of his jeans. He cut a few pieces of the yellow rat cheese onto some crackers and passed the knife to Jason. When he finished, Jason gave it to Jimmy Davis.

Jason felt very physical now. A little tired, but good from doing work that felt right, not like working in a chemical plant, which he had done. Wouldn't it be great if living could always be like this? But somehow things got twisted. Of course, he guessed the heifer would think things were not great at all. And having to put up with men midwives, too.

For the next hour the heifer did not try to labor. Twice she sat down, but the three of them tugged and kicked and got her up. It was when Bo happened to say, "Come on doll, get up. You got to hang in there," that Jason thought about Lou Beth again and her trouble. Suddenly he knew he had to see her after this chore was over.

Near dusk Bo said, "Well, I guess it's got to be the hard way. Jimmy Davis, back the jeep up till I tell you to stop." He hooked the loop over the ball of the trailer hitch when the jeep was close enough and told Jimmy Davis, "Come up easy now." The boy eased in on the clutch and the jeep strained forward.

"Come up some more." Again the straining, the taut cable. "Now hold up!" Bo slipped his glove on and followed the cable.

"The head forced through but the shoulders are too wide." Jason looked on. There was nothing he could do.

"Try it once more." Jimmy Davis tried to move forward again. "Never mind," waving him off. "We're gonna have to cut it out. Point the pickup this way and turn the lights on so I can see good."

Bo took a set of small, gleaming knives of strange shapes and spread them on the back of the jeep. "Leave the motor running."

"What can I do?" Jason asked, wanting to help.

"Just hand me things." Bo took a small curved knife that his hand covered as he went back up into the heifer. Jason wondered how Bo was going to cut the calf out without cutting the heifer.

"Jimmy Davis," Bo barked, "tighten up just a hair." He did, and Bo started cutting, sawing with the knife. "Sometimes you can cut the hide, starting around the foot and going back—just keepin on goin," he grunted. "Maybe they'll slip out. Sometimes you got to chop 'em out piece by piece." He withdrew his arm now, with the blood on his gloved hands and knife. "Come up some more, Jimmy Davis."

Suddenly the cable moved a foot and the two small gray hooves were out of the opening. The heifer was not looking around anymore, but stared through the catchpen boards out into the darkness. One or two cows came up to the other side, pushing their wet noses in her direction, trying to touch her, not able to reach her.

Bo began cutting again and once more told Jimmy Davis to tighten up. Immediately the jeep moved forward, and with only a slight pause the flesh emerged and dropped in the grass at the cow's feet, into the headlights where the blood was brilliant red.

"Well, bud, we did it," Bo said matter of factly. "Let me just put in a bolus to clean her out, and I believe she might make it. Sometimes they're tougher'n they look." He inserted the bolus in a stainless steel plunger and stuck it inside the cow. "OK, doll. There you be, good as new." His voice was soothing now, more than it was when he talked to people, Jason thought, as he patted the cow, going around to her head where he could untie her.

"Just leave her in the pen, Jimmy Davis, in case something goes wrong. See she has hay and water. And clean up all this mess aroung here, you hear? Don't want no buzzards around her."

"Yessuh."

Bo turned to Jason. "Well, bud, if we hurry we can have another cold one at Miss Ella's before she closes down."

"I got something I got to do. I'll just lend Jimmy Davis a hand and drop him off on my way back."

"Suit yourself." He tossed a shovel out of the truck and drove slowly away.

Now only the jeep lights helped them finish their job. "Damn old cow," said Jimmy Davis to nobody in particular. He slid the blade of the shovel under the shapeless afterbirth on the grass. The cow ignored him as she ignored the dumb face of another cow still staring at her through the planks of the pen. He started toward a nearby gully, and Jason dragged the lifeless calf behind.

"I'm going to need a hand with this calf," said Jason. With one on the front feet and one on the back, they swung the lifeless body into the darkness below.

Back at the catchpen, Jimmy Davis picked up the beer bottles and tipped each one to drain the last drop. Jason patted the cow on the back a couple of times and started toward the jeep, hoping he could find Lou Beth.